THREADS
More Stories from a New York Life

Other Books by Steven Schrader

What We Deserved: Stories from a New York Life
Arriving at Work
On Sundays We Visit the In-Laws
Crime of Passion

THREADS
More Stories from a New York Life

Steven Schrader

Hanging Loose Press
Brooklyn, New York

Copyright © 2012 by Steven Schrader

Published by Hanging Loose Press, 231 Wyckoff Street, Brooklyn, NY 11217-2208. All rights reserved. No part of this book may be reproduced without the publisher's written permission, except for brief quotations in reviews.

Hanging Loose thanks the Literature Program of the New York State Council on the Arts for a grant in support of the publication of this book.

www.hangingloosepress.com

Printed in the United States of America
10 9 8 7 6 5 4 3 2 1

Acknowledgments: A number of these stories first appeared in *The Reading Room, Hanging Loose*, and the on-line magazine *Per Contra*. One short section was published in the book *Crime of Passion*.

For their support and encouragement I'd like to thank Carol Conroy, Barbara Milton, Sybille Pearson, Phyllis Raphael, Louise Rose, and Ray Silver. I'd also like to thank everyone at Hanging Loose Press for their continued support: Donna Brook, Marie Carter, Bob Hershon, Mark Pawlak, and, particularly, Dick Lourie, who gave the book its final shape with his imaginative and helpful editing.

Author photo by Marvin Silver

Library of Congress Cataloging-in-Publication Data available on request.
ISBN: 978-1-934909-27-0

Contents

I	9
II	41
III	79
Coda	99

To Bob Hershon and Dick Lourie

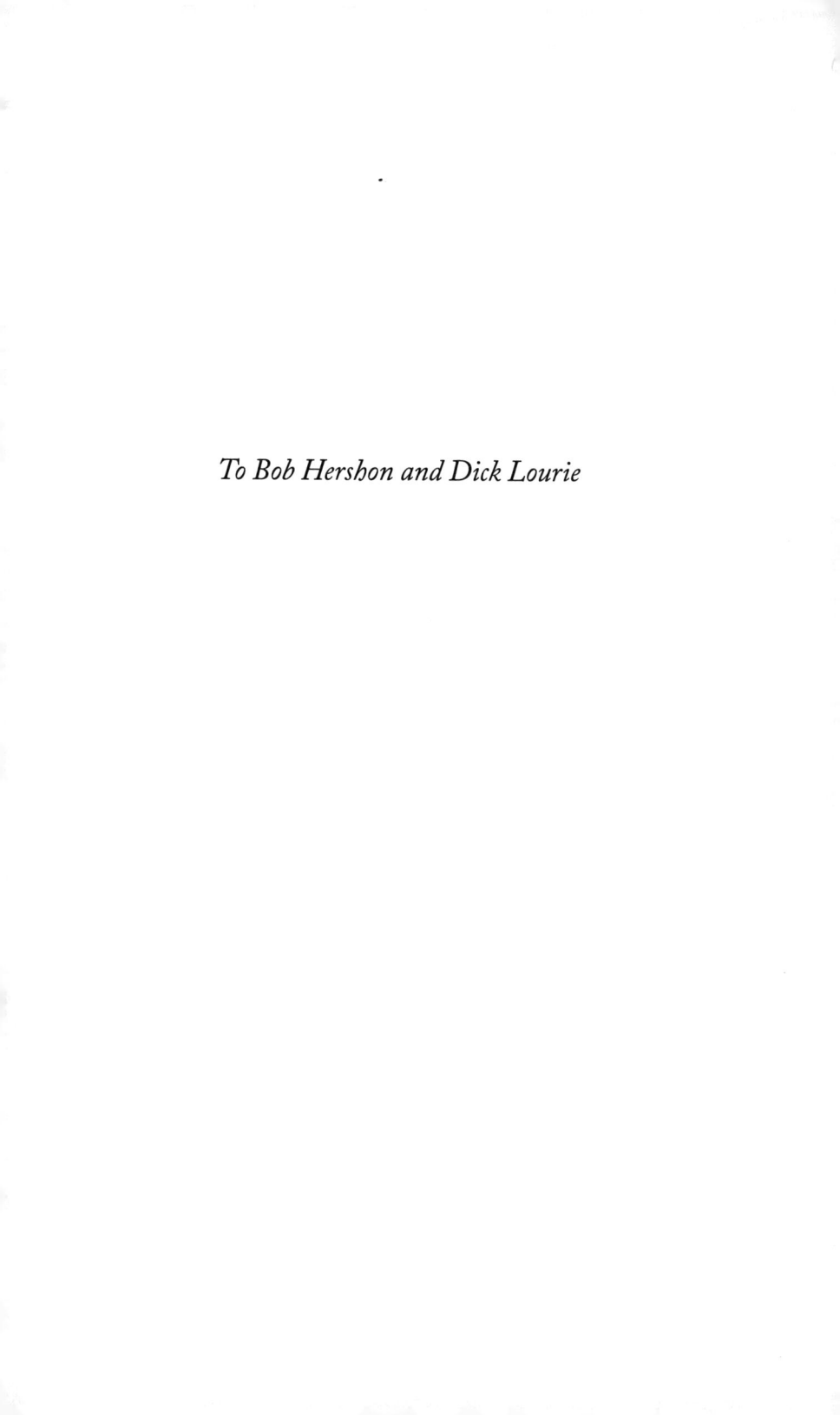

I

At the age of seven my two best friends were Joey Goldman and Kenny Klein. Joey was thin and ethereal, with straw-like blond hair. He was a good athlete but too thin and slight to have much power when he hit a ball or tried to tackle someone. There was something saintly about Joey. Walking down the street on the way to the candy store, he might bring up subjects like God or death in an offhand way, as if such things were constantly on his mind. Later he'd offer to share his candy bar with Kenny or me. He was dreamy and absent-minded, and exasperated his family. My mother said Joey was too good for this life.

Kenny was straightforward and a good athlete but without humor or lightness. Both of us courted Joey, sensing that he possessed a goodness we wanted to be close to.

My apartment house was at 660 Fort Washington Avenue; Joey's, just up the street, was at 720, the next to last building before Fort Tryon Park. Kenny lived a few blocks away on Cabrini Boulevard, so at the end of the day I usually ended up walking Joey home, past my house up to his. We'd reach his apartment house and then, unable to part, Joey would walk me home, and when we got to my building I'd insist on walking him home again. There was always something more to talk about. But our mothers had dinner waiting so finally Joey would enter his lobby, appear at the living-room window of his second-floor apartment, which faced the street, and wave goodbye to me.

When I was eight I went away to summer camp and wrote a postcard to Joey. Camp is okay, I said, then listed the batting order of our softball team, the Royals. It was my way of staying in touch with the neighborhood. I loved camp but I loved my neighborhood even more. On my return at the end of August, I ran to the schoolyard of P.S. 187, right across the street from my house, kneeled down, and kissed the cement. Washington Heights was the best place in the world and Kenny and Joey were my best friends.

When I was thirteen my family moved downtown and I lost touch with both my friends. Now that I was an outsider I couldn't bear traveling uptown to see them. By then Joey had started falling behind in school. He was left-handed and his handwriting—an important skill in grade school—was sloppy. He was also unorganized and didn't pay attention in class. Nowadays he might be diagnosed as having a learning disability, but then he was thought of as being lazy.

After graduating from P.S. 187 Joey and Kenny both went to a small private high school in Riverdale where Kenny was elected captain of the baseball team. He attended Cornell and eventually became a stockbroker. When my brother met him in the street one day in the late '50s, Kenny introduced himself as Kenneth, gave my brother his business card, and offered to advise him on buying stocks. He said that Joey had dropped out of college after one semester and taken a job with the New York City Parks Department. He was still living in his parents' apartment and working just down the block in Fort Tryon Park.

And that was the last I heard. I had the feeling that things weren't going to get better for Joey. On my occasional visits to the old neighborhood and Fort Tryon Park, I walked by the windows of his old apartment. The blinds were always drawn. I wondered if he was still there, but I wasn't sure I wanted to find out.

And then recently, sixty years after I'd left the neighborhood, I met a woman who lived at 720 Fort Washington Avenue, so I asked her about Joey. What a coincidence, she said. Two years before, she and her family had moved from a smaller apartment in the building to his, after he'd gone to an assisted living residence. So I understood that Joey had remained in the building all his life, slowly deteriorating over the years. By the time this woman moved in there he barely went out and had stopped speaking to anyone. He was cared for by a visiting nurse service, and on sunny days would occasionally be taken outside in a wheelchair. I remembered when we were boys, Joey waving at me from his front window in the evening. I was sorry that I had passed the building sometimes over the years, but had never rung the buzzer and tried to see him. I'd had my own ups and downs, been married, divorced, and then remarried again, but at least I'd had a life. I wasn't sure Joey had ever had one. I imagined him sitting behind the blinds, thinking of God and death.

***

I took my first writing class in the summer of 1954 at Cornell, after my sophomore year at New York University. I drove up to Ithaca with a friend who was a Cornell student during the school year. With six or seven other of his fraternity brothers, we stayed in their frat house. No one chipped in for anything. When the toilet paper ran out we used newspapers.

My professor was Baxter Hathaway, the founder of *Epoch*, a respected literary magazine. He was a thin, craggy-faced man, a cigarette constantly in his mouth. He wore a sport jacket with leather patches on each sleeve and drove an old car with a rope tied around one door to keep it closed. I preferred my friend's shiny new Buick convertible.

I wrote a story about a middle-aged man who, just as he was about to die, discovered the Meaning of Life. Hathaway said it was an admirable effort, but that I should take a look at Tolstoy's "The Death of Ivan Ilyich"; he suggested I try something a little less ambitious. Did he think I could become a writer, I asked. Hard to say, he answered. You just have to keep trying.

In the fall at NYU I took a writing course with Maurice Baudin, Jr., whose father was the chairman of the French department. Baudin, Jr. wore a bow tie and had a cutting sense of humor. His master's thesis had been on Somerset Maugham. He believed in the well-made story; his own work got published in *The Saturday Evening Post* and *Collier's*. He advised me to learn to type. I bought a Royal portable and a typing instruction book. I memorized the letters but didn't bother with most of the other keys. To learn how to punctuate dialogue, I read Hemingway. Because I was nervous and excited about the class, I would walk the eight flights of stairs to class, avoiding the crowded elevators. Baudin, Jr. asked us to write five stories a semester; at each session he would read the best ones—anonymously—out loud. After a while the students got to know one another's style and could tell who the author was.

I took Baudin Jr's. course for four semesters. I loved hearing my stories read out loud to the class. My main rival was Simone Hirsch, who was a year behind me. As a child she had escaped with her family from Austria to England before World War II, and spent the war there. Simone was small, had frizzy brunette hair, and wore dowdy clothes. We started having coffee together in the cafeteria after class. Her voice was beautiful and rich, with just the trace of an English accent. "It's not fair that I have to wear clothing," Simone said to me one day. "I look much better naked."

She lived in South Orange, New Jersey, so I borrowed my father's Cadillac to go out on dates with her. She told me that whenever she mentioned me to her family she referred to me as "The Cadillac." Her father worked in a factory. On Sundays she listened to Bach with him. One night we had sex in the Cadillac at a local park. As we were buttoning up, a policeman shined his flashlight at us and told us to leave.

"With people getting robbed and killed all the time," Simone complained as we drove away, "is that all he has to do?"

One of her stories was about a young girl in England during the war being lured into the woods by a man who gives her a small, cracked mirror in return for letting him touch her under her clothing. The narrator's description of the incident is matter-of-fact. The story was published in a literary magazine in the Midwest.

During spring break of my senior year, I brought Simone

to a bar in the Village to meet my friend Alan Berkowitz from Dartmouth. After taking one look at him she refused to speak to him. In the car on the way home she told me that Alan's teeth were too big, that he was overripe. "He's my best friend," I told her, but she just stared out the window. Simone and I broke up at the end of the semester. Years later I heard that she had had two children and died of cancer at thirty-five. It was hard to believe. I had been certain she was going to become a famous writer.

***

Occasionally my mother would take my brother and me half a dozen blocks from Fort Washington Avenue downtown to 181st Street and Broadway to have lunch at Horn and Hardart's Cafeteria or at the big Chinese restaurant nearby. When we reached 181st Street, a wide, crowded boulevard lined with stores and the movie theaters I sometimes went to with my friends, I felt like I was entering a big city. The biggest movie theater was the RKO Coliseum on Broadway, which played first-run films. Further east were The Heights, The Lane, The Gem, and The Empress—This was the oldest and most rundown of the theaters, where your shoes stuck to the gum on the floor and the occasional mouse rushed by.

My friends and I usually ended up at one of the smaller theaters to see the cartoons and serials they showed in addition to the double feature, but sometimes we went to the Coliseum to catch someone like Danny Kaye in Up in Arms *or Sid Caesar in* Tars and Spars. *I remember being convulsed at Caesar's routine about fighter pilots in World War II, with the American pilot smiling as his plane glided smoothly along; meanwhile the German plane made harsh, irritating sounds and the pilot ranted guttural-sounding nonsense. My friends and I imitated Caesar for weeks afterwards.*

Trolleys still ran on 181st Street and I was fascinated at the sparks of electricity from the overhead wires, which powered the trolley cars. This was also the only street in the neighborhood with traffic lights.

Except when we went to the movies, my friends and I played outside all weekend, in the street or the schoolyard, or just down the block in Fort Tryon Park, with only a short break to go home for lunch. We did this even in the winter when the wind whirled in from the Hudson and our hands turned numb from the cold. Once I remember Joey being blown about by gusts of wind and two of us grabbing him because we were afraid he'd float away. We would play outside until it grew too dark to see.

And yet, walking back from lunch on 181st Street with my brother and mother, I always felt tired and trailed behind them. My brother was almost four years older and he and my mother talked about things at lunch I didn't understand, seeming to ignore me. One time I sat down on the sidewalk and refused to go on.

"I'm tired," I shouted; I started crying.

"What a baby," my brother said, looking back at me.

"We'll just have to leave him behind," my mother said, and the two of them continued walking. I cried even harder, but they kept on. Finally, afraid they might really desert me, I got up and ran after them

"Oh, so you *can* *keep up with us,*" my mother said, taking my hand as I caught up to her. My brother made a face at me behind her back and pretended to wipe a tear from his eye.

When we reached Fort Washington Avenue we turned and walked up the steep hill to where it peaks at 183rd Street. I stayed in step with them the rest of the way home, determined not to fall behind.

***

I met Lenny at the University of Michigan in the fall of 1956. We were both graduate students in English, and he already knew everyone. Austin Warren, the respected literary critic, made Lenny his teaching assistant; the two of them would spend hours at Warren's house drinking bourbon and discussing Henry James. Lenny was also friendly with Milford and Durwood, two young black guys who didn't attend the university but were part of the scene. They played bongos and sold pot at parties.

Lenny had many girlfriends. One, Mary Jane, an attractive

blonde from a small Michigan town, taught a freshman English class. Most of her students were football players. According to Lenny, she was sleeping with one of them and intending to have sex with the rest; and, after that, perhaps the whole team.

Lenny's friend Mel was a university psychologist. One night he had counseled a student in her dorm, after she threatened to commit suicide. Now they were engaged. Mel was in his thirties, from Brooklyn, a little pudgy and a smooth talker. Liz was another Midwestern blonde—Mel said he loved her, but he worried that she was a replica of all the gentile blondes on the campus, who looked as if they had been forged in a factory that mass-produced Midwestern shiksas. A week before the wedding he flew to Miami Beach for a bachelor weekend. He slept with a couple of Jewish girls, just to make sure he wanted to go through with it. Liz was still the best, Mel said afterwards, and he married her.

One day Lenny went into a men's clothing store in downtown Ann Arbor, tried on an overcoat and walked out wearing it. He stole dozens of books about existentialism from the library, which he justified by saying that it was all right to steal from corporations, businesses and universities. Another time he was the lookout for Milford and Durwood, who pretended to be movers, and carried a couch from the student lounge to their apartment.

I was supposed to be working toward a master's degree that combined creative writing and English, but the only course I attended regularly was the writing seminar taught by Arno Bader. In his fifties with short, neat white hair, he always wore a suit and tie and, though he was a decent man, didn't seem to know much about writing.

When I told Professor Bader I was thinking of leaving school to work for my father in the dress business, he said that sometimes he regretted not going into his own family's furniture store in Grand Rapids.

Lenny thought going to work for my father was a good idea. I could work a few years, make lots of money and then write for the rest of my life. Lenny wanted to write a novel but first he needed a trade to support himself. His father was a barber on the Lower East Side and money was tight in his family.

The real reason I attended writing class was because Miya Kim was in it. She had come with me, along with a few other friends, on my 21st birthday to the Tinker Bell, a huge student hangout. If you came in on your birthday and presented proof that you had reached legal drinking age, they served you a free pitcher of beer.

Miya was tiny and weighed about ninety-five pounds. She was twenty-nine but looked much younger. Before coming to the University of Michigan, she had spent several years studying in Paris. Her father was a prominent Korean poet who wanted his daughter to see the world and become educated in Western literature and culture.

One of the other students in our writing class, a Korean War veteran, told me that in Korea all the women looked like Miya. They were a dime a dozen, he said. But the night of my birthday party when I picked her up at the private house where she rented a small room, and watched her walk gracefully down the stairs in a short, black silk dress, I was entranced. I didn't care what anyone thought; soon I stopped going to parties with Lenny and started seeing Miya most nights.

During the day I threw a football around with my roommate Bernie, who was also from New York. Bernie had a fellowship in comparative literature, and, like me, wasn't going to most of his classes. Extremely shy, and proud of his high IQ, he seemed to know everything about literature. He wrote class papers about books without having to read them. Bernie was also thinking about leaving school, but wasn't sure what to do next.

In the evening I would pick up Miya in my brother's Oldsmobile, which I had driven to Michigan, and take her out to dinner. Then we'd park in the arboretum, where there were just a few other widely spaced darkened cars, and make love in the front seat.

Neither of us was very experienced but Miya was sweet and loving. She said she felt like I was her younger brother. Before this, except with Simone, I'd usually had to convince the girl to go beyond petting and then apologize afterward for taking advantage of her. I was young and enjoyed being able to have sex whenever I felt like it. Miya was always happy to accommodate me. Soon I took her for granted; I didn't realize how difficult her life was. Having little money, she had to economize on food, besides which she suffered from migraine headaches. Her father had first shipped her off to Paris, demanding that she learn French; now he wanted her to switch languages, to study literature and write stories in English. When she hinted sometimes how hard things were, I became impatient and didn't listen.

At Christmas vacation, realizing that I was going to fail all my courses except the writing seminar, I dropped out of school and returned home. Lenny left in June. He moved in with a girlfriend and began writing stories that got published in literary magazines. Ten years later, he was nominated for a National Book Award. By then he had started mailing the books about existentialism back to the library at the University of Michigan.

Miya applied to the University's PhD program in English; I sent her my undergraduate literature textbook to help her prepare for the entrance exam. We exchanged letters for a while until I stopped writing. A year later she mailed the textbook back. That was the last I heard from her.

***

The first time I remember leaving Washington Heights and visiting a downtown apartment was when I was around eight or nine. We went to my Uncle Abe and Aunt Isabelle's Passover Seder. Their building on West 86th Street seemed grand to me, with its canopy, two uniformed doormen, and antique tables and chairs in the lobby. During dessert my father trotted me out to sing, as he usually did with company. I managed fairly tuneful versions of "Don't Fence Me In" and "Mairzy Doats," which, out of shyness, I sang from the hallway.

Then, after the applause, he encouraged me to speak up for the poor,

17

something I did at home that seemed to come naturally to me when I was young. I proclaimed that we should give money to beggars in the street and that workers should receive a good salary and that Negroes should be treated equally. The adults roared with praise and laughter. A little Bolshevik, they said. Both my Uncle Abe and my father were clothing manufacturers; the other men also worked in business. The women wore expensive silk dresses and gold jewelry. Everyone kissed me, pinched my cheek, and made a fuss over me. I sincerely did want to help the poor, but even more I liked the attention I got for my precocious leftist stance.

Thirty years later, after separating from my wife, I sublet an apartment in the same building from an acquaintance who went to live with her boyfriend in the Midwest. The building didn't seem as grand to me then: The doormen were old and moved slowly; the furniture in the lobby looked as if it could use some dusting.

At this time New York was in a state of decline—Homeless people, beggars, and addicts roamed the streets and slept in parks and on sidewalks. Like everyone else, I passed them by and wished they would go away.

***

When I returned to New York from Michigan, I decided not to go immediately into my father's dress business, but to keep pursuing in some way the idea of being a writer. I went to work for Fairchild Publications, a publishing conglomerate on 13th Street, just east of Fifth Avenue. I was hired as a copyboy at *Home Furnishings*, a trade journal that covered furniture and decorations. This was the first step to becoming a reporter there or at one of the other Fairchild trade magazines. I soon discovered the reporters were a disgruntled lot, for the most part frustrated writers doing what they considered to be hackwork—assembling manufacturers' press releases into articles for the industry. Ben Lipson, a dark-haired, handsome man about ten years older than me, spent his weekends writing scripts with a friend, hoping to break into TV.

Another reporter, Joanne, a pretty, hard-drinking woman from Oklahoma, had already given up trying to write her novel. She told Ben and me that most writing was induced by glandular conditions, so that as a person grew older, the impulse to write usually ceased.

I had a crush on Margaret, a reporter from Boston in her mid-thirties, who wore woolen suits and elegant blouses, lots of jewelry and makeup. One day at lunch I told her I liked older women and let her know I would probably end up working in the dress business for my father. She led me on for a while, even went out with me once, but wouldn't let me kiss her goodnight in the hallway of her small Village apartment. "I'm too old for you," she said. "You're just a boy."

Would she like me if were older, I asked. "Yes," she said wearily. "You're attractive, but you're too young."

By saying those magic words—that I was attractive—she had given me the assurance I needed. Now I could think of myself as being tragically and hopelessly in love with an older woman. By the next week I had recovered enough to ask out a cheerful Bennington student who was finishing up her three-month work period at Fairchild's. She too had a reason not to date me, a boyfriend at Dartmouth.

I became friendly with George, another copy boy who, like me, wanted to be a writer. He was thin, wore thick glasses and showed me stories he had written about his father, a waiter in Miami. The father took pride in his work at the restaurant, while the narrator struggled with embarrassment at his father's profession. The stories were flat and I criticized them fairly harshly. Not enough detail, I told George. They needed a more heightened conflict.

***

In the third grade I admired Betty McBride and drew a Valentine's Day card for her during art period. Betty had dark hair and white, luminous skin, rosy cheeks, and a sweet, gentle manner. She

19

lived a few blocks away from me, which in Washington Heights was like a few miles. Most of the children I hung out with were from the apartment houses near where I lived. After school, boys from all over the neighborhood played together in the schoolyard. The only girls I had anything to do with outside of school were the Foxman twins from the next building and Trudy, the one girl who could hold her own with boys in schoolyard games. Years later when I met Trudy in the Village, she had short hair and was dressed like a man.

In class I couldn't stop staring at Betty. After a while her friends noticed and started whispering and giggling. When Miss Costello gave them her annoyed look, they quieted down immediately.

I worked on my card with feverish inspiration. First I cut a square out of thick drawing paper and folded it over twice to make four sides. Then I rounded the edges into wavy shapes and drew flowers and clouds. Finally I made a heart with an arrow through it. I wrote "I Love You" and left it unsigned.

As we lined up to leave for lunch I slipped my card into Betty's desk. In the afternoon as we reached our seats I watched her pick up the card and smile and show it to her friends, who burst out laughing and pointed to me. I stared straight ahead, trying to look innocent.

"We know who sent this," they called over to me.

"Sent what?" I asked.

"We know it was you. You're in love with Betty."

Since I couldn't think of anything to say, I just looked at them and blushed. I saw Betty watching me; our eyes met and she smiled. I could feel my heart beat faster. It was true. I was in love with her. I wondered what would happen next.

Not knowing what to say to a girl, I kept my distance. Her friends teased me for a few days and then stopped. By the end of third grade, with nothing to show for it, my crush wore off. Within a few years Betty grew chubby and developed acne, but sometimes I would remember how she was in the third grade with her white skin and red cheeks as she held my Valentine's Day card and smiled at me. I could still feel my blood rush.

***

Working at Fairchild, I was back living at home, wanting to find my own place and do my own writing, but it was hard to imagine living in some dingy apartment. I still barely knew how to do my own laundry and take care of myself. One night at dinner my mother told me that a man had to plan ahead in life, had to find the kind of work that would pay for braces on his children's teeth. I accepted this as a goal, even though I didn't even have a girlfriend, let alone a child.

At night when I went to sleep in my large, comfortable bedroom in the bed that folded into a daytime sofa, I wondered if I would ever find a woman to love. I didn't belong to any circle or network, and had few of my own friends. When someone called once inviting me to a singles discussion group at the nearby synagogue, I was offended by the thought of meeting people solely because they were Jewish. "Who gave you my name?" I asked, and said I wasn't interested. But afterwards I was sorry I hadn't accepted. I would at least have been with other people, even if they were all fellow Jews.

**

All the boys in Washington Heights were crazy about baseball. In the off-season we played basketball in the schoolyard and tackle football on the lot next to the schoolyard, but baseball was king, and especially the Yankees. One year Red Rolfe, the Yankee third baseman, rented an apartment on Cabrini Boulevard—players' salaries were modest then—and his son attended P.S. 187. The boy was small and unathletic, but when I struck him out in a softball game I felt I had vanquished his father. My friends and I dreamed of one day playing for the Yankees, even though we never played hardball, since there were no dirt fields.

My friend Kenny's father had gotten to know some of the Yankee players through his business as an insurance salesman. One day he arranged for Allie Reynolds to come to their house and sign autographs for Kenny's friends. Reynolds, then a star pitcher, was an impressively large man, part American Indian, and known as the Superchief. Years later Kenny himself was scheduled for a tryout with the Yankees, while he was still in college, but during his junior year a knee injury ended his baseball career.

I envied Kenny for having a father who had been born in America and was acquainted with famous athletes. My father was from Poland: He had no interest in baseball or any of the sports I was familiar with, and was never much home anyway. I hated his European accent. He knew jujitsu and would sometimes lock his arms around my head and throw me to the ground to demonstrate the art of self-defense, but I was unimpressed.

Why don't you take me to Yankee games," I kept pleading, "like Kenny's father?"

Finally, he agreed to go with me, so one sunny, clear, cool Sunday in late September we took a cab to Yankee Stadium and bought box seats behind home plate. We had a perfect view of the pitcher and could hear the smack of the ball in the catcher's mitt. That weekend a couple of players—including Yogi Berra—had been called up from the Newark Bears, the Yankee Triple A farm team. Yogi got a few hits, and caught on with the fans right away. I loved being there. I tried to explain the rules to my father, but he was bored; a few times he closed his eyes. He worked long hours and Sunday was his only day off. As the game progressed the shadows behind home plate grew darker and the air became chilly. "We should have sat out there," my father said, pointing to the centerfield bleachers, which were still in the sun.

"You can't see anything from there, it's too far out," I said, exasperated at his lack of enthusiasm and his foreignness. "You don't know anything."

My father didn't answer. He sat patiently until the game was over; after the crowd had thinned out we left and took a cab home.

***

While I was at Fairchild I rented a furnished room, a studio on 77th Street off Columbus Avenue, for ten dollars a week. It was large and sunny. The "kitchen" consisted of a hot plate and a small sink; the bathroom was in the hall. The owner, an older, gruff man, lived on the first floor. "Are you sure you really want the room?" he asked. I assured him I did, shook hands on it and gave him two weeks' rent. Still living at home, two blocks away on Central Park West, I thought of the studio as a place to write and also where I could invite the women I was hoping to meet. I didn't feel quite ready to leave home entirely. My mother fussed over me and would offer to make a meal for me whenever I came in. We would eat in the little breakfast room with light blue walls. After dinner I'd sit at the kitchen table while my mother washed the dishes, which I would dry. Lizzie, the maid, did my laundry every week.

The first few nights I walked over to 77th Street after dinner with my notebook and a book to read, but the lights were dim and the furnishings cheap and impersonal. I left after a short time, feeling depressed. By the end of the first week I realized I couldn't stand going there and on Saturday afternoon I slipped the key under the landlord's door with a note saying that something had come up and that I would no longer be needing the room.

After three months at Fairchild, I was offered a job as a reporter for *Home Furnishings*. When I spoke to Ben Lipson about it, he advised me to go to work for my father instead. "You're crazy to stay here," he said. "This is a dead-end place. Everyone wants to get out, but they don't have the opportunity you do."

I followed his advice and turned the job down, but my real reason was different, one I could barely admit to myself. I didn't have the confidence to make it as a reporter at Fairchild's, even though everyone complained about how boring and stupid and unchallenging a place it was. Deep down, I didn't believe I could accomplish anything by myself. I needed to be near my father's power at work, the way I needed the security of my mother's care at home. I was twenty-two and still a child.

***

My friends and I hung out in the schoolyard as much as we could—in the morning before the bell rang and then again during lunch hour after gobbling down a quick sandwich at home. Then at recess we'd go back out so the boys could have their punchball game while the girls jumped rope or played jacks. After school we'd rush home for cookies and milk and then return to play softball or basketball until it grew dark.

Once after school we were getting ready for a basketball game. Meanwhile, across the schoolyard, a softball game was under way. Our basket was actually in deep center field. My friends and I were joking around until, suddenly, they all scattered in different directions. I remained in place, unable to move, like in a dream, wondering why everyone had disappeared. Then a well-hit fly ball bounced off the top of my head and I fell to the ground.

I immediately remembered the time a few years before when I hit my head against a tree while sledding and my mother had rushed me to the hospital, worried that the blow might prove fatal. The next day, a friend had told me that blood clots sometimes kicked in years afterwards, and I was still worried about it.

Because I knew that this time, at the least, my mother would forbid me to go out and play after school, I decided not to tell her. By the next morning I felt I would probably survive for a while, the way I had lived through the sledding accident. As I got older, though, an occasional slight headache or twinge of pain would remind me of the sled smashing into the tree or the softball hitting my head, and of my friend's observation: I'd wonder if I was finally about to die. One of these days, of course, I will.

***

After quitting Fairchild I began working as a salesman for my father in the dress business. The showroom was usually bustling, and I found it hard to greet buyers as if I had known them all my life, the way the other salesmen did. Behind the scenes they were cynical and sarcastic, but in the showroom they barreled ahead with confidence and bravado and the utmost sincerity.

To complicate matters, often as I showed someone a dress I became dizzy and believed I was dying. It wasn't until years later, when my sixteen-year old daughter was diagnosed with anxiety attacks and given breathing exercises to help her relax, that I was able to identify what I had suffered from. At the time I simply knew I was subject to a kind of craziness that I had to conceal from others.

Once the salesmen realized that I presented no threat to take over their accounts, they tolerated me; some even took me under their wing and instructed me on the art of selling dresses. My father was too busy to notice me. When he had first arrived in New York from Europe, he had said to himself that America was a place anyone could succeed in if he worked hard and seized opportunities. And he had proved himself right. But I wasn't in any condition to seize opportunities; I was merely trying to get through the day without falling down and dying. Often I had to grab onto a rack of dresses or one of the small tables in the showroom to steady myself.

During Market Week each season, when a new line of dresses was displayed at fashion shows twice a day, my job was to hand every model an index card that described the dress she was wearing and quoted the price. I would stand outside the models' room with a stack of index cards in the right order and give the appropriate one to each woman as she stepped into the showroom. The models would in turn give the cards to our publicity lady, who passed the information to the buyers in the showroom. Considered innocent and naïve, I was chosen for this task because none of the other salesmen could be trusted not to say suggestive things to the models or slip in feels as they rushed past.

Secretly, I was infatuated with them as I stood outside the small, narrow, crowded models' room and peeped through the curtains, pretending to arrange the index cards. The models were slender, outgoing women in their 20s and 30s. Maria, our house model, who worked full time for us, was a beautiful, dark-haired, unpretentious woman in her mid-twenties. She'd been a high school swimmer in Wilmington, Delaware, and had broad shoulders and a thin waist. When she first came to New York, she had been introduced by a friend to a large, talkative man named Vinnie, whom she began dating. He took her to different restaurants in the Village, where he received special treatment and seemed to know everyone. When Maria discovered that he was collecting protection money for the Mafia, she tried to break up with him. She wanted to start seeing Richie, one of the salesmen in the company. But Vinnie called Richie at work one day and threatened to break his legs. So Maria was stuck with him.

Parading past the buyers, the models, with their stylized walk, were elegant and graceful. I was shocked to see some of them stuff pads around their hips and slip falsies into their brassieres as they prepared for a show. Once it was under way, there was controlled pandemonium as the seven or eight models yanked off their dresses and pulled on new ones while the designer and her assistant frantically selected appropriate shoes and jewelry for them. The models flirted with me and told me they liked my dimples. By the second day of Market Week I felt comfortable enough to joke back with them. I was sad when each show was over for the day and I had to fold and put away the extra chairs, and help wait on the crowd of buyers.

Then Market Week was over and the showroom returned to normal. Every day was boring, with nothing to look forward to except my periodic dizzy spells. A few times I saw one of the models in the elevator of our building or in the street and we smiled and said hello.

Soon after one of those Market Weeks, Maria's boyfriend was arrested by the FBI, indicted, and sentenced to fifteen years in prison. Maria married Richie. They moved to Fort Lee, New Jersey and she left modeling to raise a family.

After a year in my father's business I was drafted into the army. I didn't try for a deferral, even though I was afraid I wouldn't make it through basic training. But to my surprise I was able, without feeling dizzy or fearful, to fire my rifle accurately, throw a live grenade fifty feet, and crawl under barbed wire while machine gun fire whizzed by ten feet over my head. As things turned out, basic training was much easier than selling dresses.

***

Our 4th *grade teacher, Miss Bertzel, helped us plant vegetables in the Victory Garden on a tiny plot of land behind the fence at the Fort Washington Avenue entrance of P.S. 187. She was a kindly, white-haired woman who assured us that our efforts would help win the war. Double-decker buses and cars passed us on the street only occasionally. Most people didn't yet own automobiles.*

My parents didn't have a car, so on Sundays we would all go for rides in the country with some of my father's business associates. Often it was with Charlie Goodman, the production man for a large dress company, and his short, heavy wife Betsy. We'd go up the West Side Highway and onto the Taconic, parallel to the Hudson River. Then my father would buy everyone lunch at the Red Apple Rest or at Orseck Brothers restaurant. My brother and I brought mitts and a ball so we could have a catch outside while the grownups talked over coffee.

We also went with my father's insurance man, Nathan Langberg and his wife and their Scottie dog, which they sometimes brought up to our apartment before we set out. One time the dog kept pacing near the door of our bedroom, which my brother and I had closed so it would stay with us. Finally it squeezed next to the radiator and peed. Oh, that's why you wanted to get out, we said apologetically to the dog, and wiped up the pee with paper napkins.

Frequently we drove with the Marmelsteins, Dave and his wife Hank. He was the president of the Better Dress Association and helped my father find work for his dress factory. Hank was a brash, talkative woman who wore lots of necklaces and bracelets and worked for Olson and Brown, an accounting firm that did the books for my father's company. Max Olson, the co-owner of the firm, was also part owner of the camp in the Poconos where my brother and I went each summer. The Marmelsteins were heavy smokers and Hank saved the silver foil wrappers from their cigarette packs, which I rolled into giant balls and brought to school for the war effort.

My mother bought black market meat and squeezed it in a press so that I could have a glass of blood every day. She was afraid I would get sick and die, the way my sister had, the year before I was born—or else suffer the fate of her two brothers, who had died during the influenza epidemic in Europe.

My father secured a contract to manufacture WAC uniforms and did so well that he sent my mother and my brother and me to Florida each winter for years, starting in 1943. Much later he told me that, because of wartime rationing, he'd had to bribe the head of the Woolen Bureau to obtain enough material to keep up with his orders. That was the way the world worked, he said.

In the empty lot just north of the schoolyard, my friends and I acted out battles between the Americans and the Germans. We told jokes in German and Japanese accents. I didn't find out until years later that my father's sister had been killed by German soldiers and that when her husband wouldn't give up his coat to the Nazis, he was torn apart by dogs.

***

After basic training, I spent twenty months as a company clerk at Fort Dix. During that time I processed seven or eight cycles of trainees, altogether around fifteen hundred men. Most of them were unmemorable in that they did what they had to in order to get through basic training and go on to advanced training at another base. But usually one or two trainees would be bed wetters or just difficult, like George Grant, who stole a box of clothes hangers from the supply room and tried to sell them to other recruits. He was the kind of kid who was always looking for an angle, but then would act so stupidly that he almost seemed to want to get caught. I was sure that as an adolescent he must have been frequently suspended from school. I typed up his discharge papers, under what was called Section 8—unfit due to psychological problems—a label that, we were told, would doom the recipient to lifelong failure.

The most memorable of my Section 8s was Barry Malzberg, a big, hairy, ungainly New Yorker with thick glasses, who had been drafted right out of college. He couldn't do anything right, partly because of bad coordination and partly because of his arrogant attitude. Once he was sent to the orderly room as punishment and told to sweep the floor. He started pushing the broom around and stirring up dust haphazardly, complaining that he was a college graduate and shouldn't have to do something so menial.

Usually I left the yelling to the sergeants, an activity considered a normal part of basic training, a way to break an individual's spirit and to mould the company into a solid unit, though I'm not sure the sergeants would have put it that way. But there was something in Malzberg—maybe because he was also a Jew, or because he took such pride in his assumed intelligence and superiority—that pushed a nerve in me so that I screamed at him to sweep the fucking floor or I'd take the broom and shove it up his ass.

A year later, after my own discharge, I noticed Malzberg sitting at a desk in a classroom at the training center of the New York City Welfare Department, where I was about to begin working as an investigator. He didn't notice me and I sat on the other side of the room without saying hello. Here he seemed to stick out less than he had in the army.

Some years later I read an article about the Scott Meredith Literary Agency, which at the time handled Norman Mailer and many other well-known writers, and was shocked to discover that Malzberg was one of the company's star agents. The article mentioned that, because of a phobia about elevators, he walked up the forty-two flights of stairs to his office every morning, but that he was a brilliant editor.

He had also started to write science fiction and within a few years became well known himself. He wrote prolifically under his own name and also under several pseudonyms, publishing hundreds of books and stories and winning numerous awards. Most of his writing was done during the '70s, after which he slowed down, eventually moved to Europe and published only occasionally.

Recently I noticed that he was on a panel about the state of science fiction writing and I thought of going for old times' sake, but it was a freezing night; I never managed to leave the house. Instead I looked him up on the Internet. There were pages of articles and comments, along with several photographs. He had lost weight and was bald, with whitish sideburns, and he must have gotten contact lenses because he no longer had on those thick glasses. He was still awkward-looking, but there was something almost attractive about him, sort of a cross between Woody Allen and Isaac Asimov.

One reader said that she thought of him as brilliant and essential, but so depressing that she limited herself to one book of his a year, which she usually found at a used book store.

I was sorry I hadn't gone to hear him that night. I wondered if he would have remembered me.

***

My first summer at camp I took riding lessons, at the suggestion of my father. Growing up in Europe, he'd had his own horse, and his left wrist still ached occasionally from a fall. Two mornings a week a small group of fellow campers and I walked down a dirt hill, past the dining hall to an old stable encircled by a riding path. The first few times a counselor held onto the reins as I rode slowly around the ring. Finally, I was allowed to ride by myself. I sat straight in the saddle and swayed to the horse's motion. I knew my father would be proud of me. But when the horse began trotting I lost my balance and slipped to the ground.

The riding counselor pulled me up and brushed me off. "You're okay, son," he said. "Climb back on to show you're not afraid." He pushed me up. I clutched the reins and managed to remain on the horse for the rest of the period. I was sorry my father wasn't there to see me.

Every morning after breakfast, as we younger campers cleaned our bunks for inspection, we were visited by Aunt Mae. Round-faced and white-haired, Aunt Mae wore long cotton dresses. She washed our combs and brushes, and generally played the part of our mother away from home. Behind Aunt Mae's back, we made fun of her, feeling that she treated us like babies. We were too grown up for her and made off-color jokes to prove it. *Do you eat it with a spoon*, we'd ask one another and then break out laughing. One morning someone asked Aunt Mae if she ate it with a spoon. "Of course I do," she said. "I always eat with a spoon." We all began laughing hysterically and couldn't stop for the rest of the day. We kept repeating it: *Aunt Mae eats it with a spoon.*

In mid-July, news about a polio epidemic spread through camp. As soon as I heard about it I could feel my legs tingle and become numb. The next morning I limped to the clinic to tell Caroline the nurse that I had polio. Caroline was a young, attractive blonde, and after she examined me she shook her head and smiled. "There's nothing wrong with you," she said. "Except maybe polio on the brain." I ran back to my bunk to get ready for baseball, embarrassed about my fears but exhilarated that I wasn't doomed to die or become a cripple.

A couple of days later Billy Behrner, one of my counselors, sent me to the clinic for three Fallopian tubes. "Tell him we're all out and won't be getting any more this summer," Caroline said, rolling her eyes. I returned to the bunk to tell Billy, sensing he had sent me to the clinic as a joke, but not really minding.

Nature period was the least popular of our activities. Once a week we'd go to the nature shack and look at dry leaves or else take a walk in the woods with the nature counselor, who told us the names of trees. The only boys who enjoyed Nature were Maurice Goldberg and Shelly Cooper. Maurice liked to catch butterflies with a net and mount them. Whenever his name came up, we'd say that he was out somewhere goosing butterflies.

Shelly's father was the music director of the camp, so Shelly was forced to spend his summers there, despite his poor coordination and lack of interest in sports. The one time we paid attention in Nature was when the counselor dropped a frog into a terrarium occupied by a garter snake. The frog hopped to a corner and froze in terror while the snake slid over, darted its tongue out and shot its head forward almost faster than we could see, swallowing the frog whole. For the rest of the period we stared with fascination as the frog's body passed through the snake. The counselor explained in a dry, instructional way that this was an example of "peristalsis." We wanted to watch until the frog disappeared, but the bugle sounded for swimming and, reluctantly, we left.

On Friday nights in the rec hall before Jewish services, Mrs. Van Royen, one of the camp owners, gave long, inspirational, sermon-like speeches. She had sharp features and a regal bearing, and she wore her black hair swept back dramatically. Mrs. Van Royen warned us against the dangers of keeping food in our cubbies, except for hard candies. We instructed our parents to disguise any forbidden treats they sent us by wrapping them in plain brown paper, but sometimes our packages were opened anyway, and confiscated. When banned food was discovered, Mrs. Van Royen became enraged. "Salamis breed chipmunks in the bunks," she would screech at us in her high-pitched voice. It was almost worth having your package confiscated just to hear her carry on.

I was an outstanding athlete and tried to excel at everything, and the first few years at camp I won many awards. But then I got chubby and the other boys grew bigger and stronger. I was no longer outstanding, I had peaked too early.

***

A little over a month before I was to be discharged from the army I took a thirty-day leave to Paris on a flight from McGuire Air Force Base, the way my friend Pete Chambers had done previously. He drew me a map in red ink of his version of Paris, which was mostly the Left Bank along the Seine, with the Notre Dame Cathedral and the little hotel he had stayed at and Place Pigalle where he'd met a prostitute he had lived with for a few days and the jazz club Le Chat Qui Peche, where black American musicians hung out.

I had a good time walking around Paris and also reading Henry Miller in my hotel room, though I didn't find a prostitute to move in with. When I returned a week or so before my discharge,

Sergeant Phillips referred to me jokingly as a short-timer. He arranged for me to receive a Certificate of Achievement, which described, with many adjectives and clichés, my outstanding work as a company clerk.

He and Captain Green, the company commander, were my immediate supervisors. Captain Green was a tall, powerful black man, and a confident leader. Cleon Phillips, the white first sergeant, was from Georgia and hoped to return there as a peanut farmer when he retired. He was solidly built and cheerful and paid attention to details. Both men arrived every morning at 5AM and worked closely together to help me prepare the morning report, before the company left on training maneuvers.

My last morning in the army I shook hands with Captain Green and Sergeant Phillips as they left for the rifle range. I felt sad that I'd never see them again. At eight I reported to Central Headquarters on the other side of the base to get my Certificate of Achievement signed by the Fort Dix commander. I walked through a huge room full of clerks busily typing at their desks until I reached a sergeant outside the general's office, who told me that General Wooster wasn't expected back until later. I waited. By early afternoon I realized impatiently that if not for the damn award I would already have been back home in New York. But in truth I really did want it as proof that I had succeeded at something and also because I had been told that it would help when I looked for a job.

General Wooster arrived around four. He was a trim, straight-backed, balding man who nodded to me as I entered his office. He asked me what I was planning to do.

"I'm not sure, sir," I said, not expecting the question and not really knowing the answer.

"Well, then, you ought to re-up," he said. "You'll get a big bonus and a promotion."

For a moment I remembered my success as a company clerk and how much I liked Captain Green and Sergeant Phillips. I considered following the general's advice. But I also knew there was nothing more for me to learn in the army. "I'll have to think about it, sir," I said.

A couple of days later, on the advice of my friend Pete, I went down to the Welfare Department and filled out an application to become an investigator. Pete was already working as one in the Bronx. No one asked to see my Certificate of Achievement. A week later I was assigned to the Harlem Welfare Center on 131st Street at the East River. The large room with its rows of desks where I was to sit reminded me of Central Headquarters at Fort Dix; I felt reassured.

***

On Thanksgiving weekend, shortly before my bar mitzvah, I broke my arm playing basketball. One afternoon a few weeks later, after a visit to the doctor, I rode home on the subway. I got off at 190th *Street and started up the staircase to Fort Washington Avenue. From the top of the stairs I could look back down on the roofs of apartment houses below on Broadway, and west to the Hudson River. I liked this view. The steps were icy and I walked near the stone railing covered with snow, schoolbooks in my good hand. My left sleeve hung empty, my broken arm sheltered under my coat.*

A group of girls from Mother Cabrini High School giggled at the top of the stairs, full of nervous energy after a day of parochial school discipline. They looked alike in their dark blue outfits: coats, caps, high stockings and skirts, their satchels bulging with books.

No one liked these girls. They didn't live in our neighborhood and I had never spoken to any of them. We were sure that they had learned anti-Semitism from the Sisters. Sometimes we called them "Catholic devils."

A snowball flew past me and, with loud whoops, they bombarded me with snowballs they had hidden in their sleeves and pockets. The snowballs didn't hurt, but I felt ashamed at being hit by a bunch of girls. They kept throwing and moved closer. I scooped up snow from the railing and shaped a snowball with my one good hand.

The nearest girl put her snowballs down and shouted, "He's only got one arm. It's not fair."

They stopped. I looked at the girl who had spoken and lobbed my snowball at her. It hit her shoulder.

"Why, you little punk," she cried, jumping down the last few steps to rub a snowball on my face. When I pushed her away they all ran up and rubbed my face with snow, then poured it down my back. Then they ran into the subway. I shook the snow off and walked home.

***

At the Harlem Welfare Center I had a caseload of about seventy-five families, most of them from the St. Nicholas Housing Project in West Harlem. Doris Featherstone, my supervisor, was a light-skinned, elegant-looking black woman in her mid-forties. She gave me helpful advice about some of my clients, like the elderly Williams couple, who, besides the regular investigator, needed a visiting health care worker to look in on them and cut their nails. Mr. and Mrs. Williams were white-haired and in their late eighties. They lived in a sunny apartment with two yellow birds that chirped constantly. A tapestry depicting President Kennedy hung on the wall. The first afternoon I visited they were listening to a Yankee game. I accepted the cup of tea Mrs. Williams offered, even though I wasn't supposed to, and when I left they told me to be careful in the street. I felt more like a son or grandson than a welfare investigator.

Mrs. Featherstone also told me about Mr. Jones, an elderly blind man who lived on the first floor of a small tenement building near the St. Nicholas Projects. He had once left the burner on and started a fire in his apartment and now his nephew lived with him and took care of him. This was against welfare rules, Mrs. Featherstone explained, since the nephew didn't pay rent. "But we let it go," she said. "Otherwise we'd have to place him in an institution."

Investigators were required to visit their clients once a month, which meant they were frequently out of the office in what was called "the field." An investigator was expected to make three visits in an afternoon. I soon learned that you could make six or seven, even eight or nine, if you pushed, particularly in my case, as almost everyone lived near one another. The day after a visit you recorded your notes on a Dictaphone for a secretary to type up. What most investigators did was to record only three visits at a time and save the others for later. This meant that you had spare afternoons when you could leave the office; on the next day you would record your previous visits, dating them as if you had not taken a half-day off. In this way I was able to see lots of afternoon movies.

For many of its employees the Welfare Department was a refuge. Young college graduates like myself, who didn't know what they wanted to do in life could spend a year or two at an undemanding job while they figured things out. Then there were others for whom the Welfare Department was a permanent retreat. Jerry Levinson, who sat at a nearby desk, had served as an infantry medic in Europe during the Second World War. Afterwards, he had never gotten back into the competitive swing of things. He was a slim, handsome man about twelve years older than I was. Jerry wrote plays that didn't get produced.

Another neighbor of mine, Mildred Dunbar, was a plump, dark black woman from Mississippi, who still hoped to become an elementary school teacher, but because of her southern accent she had repeatedly failed the New York City Board of Education's speech exam. Like many of the black investigators, she was critical and suspicious of her clients, most of whom she felt were lazy and didn't deserve help.

The younger workers like myself were more on the idealistic side; we tried to give away what we could with special grants for clothing and furniture. The majority of clients were young women with children. Their cases were classified as Aid to Dependent Children (ADC), which was intended for single parents who weren't required to work because their children were under sixteen. If there was a man around it didn't pay for the woman to reveal it, since she would have her grant significantly reduced or be taken off welfare altogether. The welfare rules didn't encourage family life or even give clients any real help in finding jobs, but, like most of the young workers, I simply ignored the failings in the system. I had my own life to worry about.

What I enjoyed most about being an investigator was walking around Harlem and taking in the sights. On one block, in the middle of the seedy tenements, was a row of brownstones with well-kept gardens. Often between Fifth Avenue and Madison at 128th Street, I spotted an elderly white woman in a bright turban, with a parrot on her shoulder. There was always a lot of action in the streets, with young unemployed men standing around talking. Occasionally the police would curse at the prostitutes standing on the corners and chase them away.

I enjoyed talking to my clients and getting to know the stories of their lives. Many of the women had always depended on pleasing men to get by; they were attractive and flirtatious. I knew that a number of male investigators had sex with their clients and I sensed that to some of the women I was exotic—a young, friendly white man who liked to chat with them. One time a woman in a tight sweater pressed against me at the door and said she wanted to thank me for being so generous. Though I was attracted to her, I pulled away out of fear of getting into trouble. "I'm sorry, I've got to get back to the office," I said and scooted out.

I walked back to the welfare center and asked Mrs. Featherstone to switch my client to another caseworker. Mrs. Featherstone told me to include a description of the incident in my report. I had already decided not to make any mention of it in the client's files since I didn't want to prejudice the next investigator against her. Besides, I felt I might have led her on by my own manner, though I didn't say this to Mrs. Featherstone. Toward the end of our talk, she asked me how I was feeling about my job and if I planned to stay. Without thinking, I told her I would probably be leaving within a year. Working for the welfare department wasn't really a job for a man, I said, reflecting on what my family and friends had said, and not taking into account that Mrs. Featherstone's husband was also a supervisor at the center. She gave me a tight smile and

37

nodded. "Well, you do what's right for yourself," she said.

A few months later she was promoted to be supervisor of the intake section of the center. Not too long after that I left for a job as a street worker with gangs, at a salary that was even less than I was making at the Welfare Department, but the work seemed more interesting and worthwhile. It wasn't until years later that I thought of what I had said to Mrs. Featherstone and realized how tolerant and generous she had been to me.

***

Going on bus trips from Camp With-Wind to play basketball or baseball games against other camps, we would pass through Waymart, a tiny town of a few hundred people. Its dusty main street consisted of a few houses, a general store, and a bar. "We are now entering Waymart, Pennsylvania," we'd shout from the windows of the bus. "We are now leaving Waymart, Pennsylvania."

Waymart was within walking distance from camp and counselors went there frequently at night to drink. One night someone from town called Bill Mack a dirty Jew. Bill wasn't even Jewish but he was a weight lifter and a football player, and he knocked the man down and a brawl started. After that counselors weren't allowed to go to town on their nights off.

One sunny afternoon in the middle of the week I saw Bill walking up the hill from the boys' swimming dock with his girlfriend onto the boys' campus. They were carrying a picnic basket and a blanket and had canoed back from the island in the middle of the lake where they had spent their day off. They were both in T-shirts and bathing suits; his girlfriend had long beautiful legs. She kept touching the back of his neck and putting her arm around his shoulder. It was the first time I was certain that a couple had just had sex. Bill seemed embarrassed and pulled away, as if he wanted her to stop being so openly affectionate. I had the sense that he felt softened and domesticated by this revelation of recent intimacy with a woman. He was now a housebroken male on good behavior: no more fights in bars. The next summer the two of them returned as a married couple.

Thirteen-year-olds like myself worshipped the counselors, especially those who were good athletes. Many of them had played varsity basketball at Erasmus High School, where Al Badain, the camp head counselor, was the basketball coach. At night they sometimes played against teams from other camps. Afterwards we'd walk up the dirt road to the boys' campus, shining our flashlights on the ground so we wouldn't trip. We'd still be talking about the moves the counselors had made during the game and we'd jump around in imitation. To be an accomplished athlete was the achievement we most desired; each of us hoped to win the best athlete award at the end of the summer or at least the award for "most improved athlete." Eventually most of my bunkmates, chubby Jewish boys from Brooklyn and Long Island, became doctors and lawyers, but at the time we believed anything was possible.

***

One spring evening a few months after my discharge from the army, while I was still at the Welfare Department, I went with my friend Bernie to a concert. I had just discovered the folk music scene in Greenwich Village and was excited when I saw a notice on a lamppost that Ramblin' Jack Elliott and Jean Redpath would be performing at a diner on West 3rd Street, near Washington Square Park. I had heard of Elliott, a disciple of Woody Guthrie who had recorded some of Guthrie's songs for Folkways Records. Ramblin' Jack was actually from Brooklyn (as I found out later): His real name was Elliott Charles Adnopoz and his father was a doctor. But he was lean, wiry, handsome, looking and sounding like a cowboy. In between songs he told long, funny stories about his life and travels. I could have listened to him for hours. Jean Redpath, whom I had expected to be Native American because of her name, turned out to be a young Scottish woman making her New York debut. She was plump and pretty, with a pure, sweet voice and a seemingly endless repertoire of Scottish songs, most of them beautiful and sad.

Elliott was the featured act. Near the end of his set he looked out at the audience and said, "Hey, there's Bobby Dylan." I had just read a rave review about Dylan in the New York Times; he was about to be discovered, but at the time he was still a kid hanging around Elliott, sopping up everything he could from him. Elliott and Redpath were going to do a second show, but I felt too shy to stay. Everything I did then was related to what I feared people might think about me, and I thought it wouldn't look cool to remain sitting there as if we had nothing better to do. Bernie, who wasn't as interested in the folk scene as I was, said he didn't care one way or the other. We could have paid another five-dollar cover charge and ordered another round of coffee, but I decided to leave. Looking back, I've always regretted not staying, since I'm sure Dylan got up and sang a few songs with Elliott—that was one of the ways he learned to perform, following friends around to their gigs and joining them on stage. It turned out that I never did get to see Dylan perform live, though over the next year or so our paths crossed several times walking along West 4th Street, where I read later he lived with a girlfriend. Each time I passed him Dylan seemed preoccupied, as if he were writing a song in his head or thinking about a new move on the guitar.

After the concert that night, walking with Bernie through Washington Square Park, where folk singers performed on Sundays, I imagined playing there myself before an admiring crowd. Within a week I bought a cheap steel string guitar and started taking lessons from someone a friend recommended. I also bought a tape recorder to practice telling stories, the way Jack Elliott did. I perfected a twang that I thought sounded like his, but then got sidetracked with other things and stopped playing. Occasionally over the years I take out my guitar, struggling to play the one or two songs I still remember. I think of the night I didn't stay to hear Bob Dylan and I wonder what else I've missed all my life.

II

Starting in the 7th grade, when I was 12, my parents had sent me downtown to Hudson, a private boys' school. But of course after school I'd still come home to Washington Heights and hang out with my friends in the P.S. 187 schoolyard. One afternoon a well-thumbed copy of The Amboy Dukes was getting passed around. Pages featuring sexy passages had been folded at the top corner. I skimmed through those parts excitedly, wondering if I myself would ever have the chance to experience such bliss. A couple of weeks later my brother brought home a pornographic story one of his friends had found at a store on 42nd Street. After reading it several times with the same enthusiasm I'd had for The Amboy Dukes, I decided to write a story myself, using this one as a model.

The next day I took mine to Hudson, and offered to let classmates read it for a dime. I had few takers, so pretty soon I just let everyone read it for nothing. This story was my first attempt at writing fiction. It featured many purple passages about succulent breasts, wet vaginas, and creamy, silvery fluids. Some of the boys shook their heads in disgust, but I felt proud of it.

***

Ellen and I had met just before I went into the army. We got married in 1963. A year later I was twenty-eight, had stopped working with street gangs, and was looking for a new career. I got a job teaching English in a Bronx junior high school and enrolled in education classes at City College to qualify for a permanent license. My cousin Norman, who was an assistant principal at a another junior high school, helped me maneuver my way through the Board of Education's labyrinths to secure this first job. By coincidence I was assigned to JHS 44, where Norman himself had been a student twenty-five years earlier. He had learned to love books under the guidance of Miss Gibney, the school librarian. Norman remembered her fondly; when I started teaching at JHS 44, she was still there.

Now, however, a quarter of a century after Norman's time in junior high, white-haired and frail, she seemed hopelessly out of step with her surroundings. The building of the Cross Bronx Expressway and Co-op City had chased the lower middle class from the neighborhood; the remaining families who stayed were extremely poor. When I brought one of my classes to her for a lesson in library skills, Miss Gibney would lecture the students about the promiscuous lives they were leading. She would go on about the filth in newspapers and on television and in the movies, until the bell rang. Miss Gibney was in her late sixties, but with her hair pulled back in a bun and her high-necked dresses and plain black shoes, she seemed to come from a previous century. The students rolled their eyes and twisted in their seats while she badgered and scolded them, but, intimidated by her strangeness, her furious intensity, they remained silent.

In my regular English classes students screamed and ran around as much as they pleased, no matter how much I yelled at them. I was young and well meaning and had at first tried to be their friend, which, of course, was a terrible mistake. When we were scheduled to visit the library they begged me to let them stay in our classroom instead. "We'll be good, we promise," they pleaded. "Just don't make us listen to that old lady. She's scary."

I told them that I was sorry, but that there was no getting around it. The Board of Education, I said, insisted on teaching library skills. "It's just for one period," I would say as I marched them to the library. Then at the back of the room I would lean comfortably against the bookshelves and watch the students fall into a glassy-eyed stupor as Miss Gibney railed against alcohol, drugs and sex for the next forty minutes. It was my favorite class.

***

One evening at a party, a year or two after we had moved downtown, I met Stanley. He sat at the piano, girls crowding around him and singing along as he played tunes like "Garden in the Rain." Stanley was tall and handsome, with thick black hair plastered to his head. He wore a white shirt, a tie and a sport jacket. I asked him for the name of his piano teacher, a woman on the West Side, and we got to talking. By the end of the evening we had agreed to hang out together the following Saturday. We met then, and were walking along Broadway when two boys came up to us. The smaller, much younger boy was pointing at me. The older grabbed my arm. I had never seen either of them before. Stanley took a step back.

"You sure this is the guy?" the older boy said. "Yes, that's him," said the other. "You punched my brother in Central Park this morning," the bigger boy said. He hit me in the chest and I fell down. Having heard somewhere that you could be killed by a punch to the heart, I was afraid to fight back. Adults passed by without a word, some of them shaking their heads.

"That'll teach you," the older boy said, and they walked away.

"You were smart to stay down," Stanley said, with what I felt was a trace of disdain. He was bigger than me and I wanted to ask why he hadn't helped me. But I was new to the neighborhood and needed friends, particularly ones who, like Stanley, seemed popular. Most of my Hudson classmates were lost souls like me. We didn't pay attention in class and we cheated on exams. Saturday afternoons we sat in the balcony at the 81st Street RKO or the Loews at 83rd and made kissing

noises during love scenes. Once someone a few rows down from us looked around with irritation. I saw that it was Pat, a doorman from my building, with his ten-year-old son. Pat was a pleasant, friendly man, who lived nearby on Columbus Avenue, which at the time was full of poor tenement buildings and Irish bars. I slunk down in my seat and hoped he hadn't seen me. I dreamed of a more elevated and cultured life, reading books and also being an outstanding athlete at a more prestigious school, but in the meantime I crashed parties and chipped in with my friends for whiskey on weekends. That was why I wanted Stanley as a friend. I felt he could help me change my life, teach me how to dress like him, to play the piano and to be confident.

The next week I called Stanley's piano teacher. Soon I was clunking my way through "Garden in the Rain," but my progress seemed slow. I couldn't focus on practicing, my parents weren't interested in my playing and Stanley didn't return my phone calls. After a few months I quit lessons.

"Garden in the Rain" was the only song I remembered by heart. Sometimes at home I'd sit down in the living room and play it and imagine a group of kids standing around singing the words:

> ...'Twas just a garden in the rain
> but then the sun came out again
> and sent us happily on our way.

And for a while I'd forget how miserable I was.

***

In 1964 my father organized a luncheon to help President Johnson raise money for his election campaign against Barry Goldwater. Held at a hotel ballroom near the garment district, it was attended by union officials, dress manufacturers, and a few celebrities like Sammy Davis, Jr. At the last minute Johnson had to pull out. He sent his running mate, Hubert Humphrey, as a substitute.

Because of minor eye surgery the day before, my father wore a patch over one eye, which, along with the excitement of heading such a momentous event, made him nervous and dizzy. To calm himself he kept drinking Scotch.

In his introductory remarks he told everyone how much he admired Johnson and Humphrey, whom he called friends of the common people. I had never heard my father speak in public before; I was impressed at how well he managed to project his own immigrant experience and personality. Humphrey, who towered over my father as he approached the podium, gave him a big hug. My father stumbled slightly on his way back to the table where Ellen and I and my mother were sitting. By this time in her life my mother was never feeling well and didn't go out much, but my father had insisted she attend this event.

In contrast with my father's plainspokenness, Humphrey's oratorical style was smooth and experienced. He talked eloquently about the greatness of America—its beautiful mountains and deserts and its thriving cities. I had the feeling he had performed this speech many times before. He mentioned "the success of my good friend Abe Schrader" as an example of the opportunities America offered newcomers. When Humphrey apologized for being a poor substitute for Johnson, my father stood up and shouted, "No, no, Mr. Vice President. We're happy to have you here."

Humphrey, who had obviously meant the words rhetorically, seemed surprised and a little amused by my father's outburst. "Thank you, Abe, I appreciate your encouraging words," he said and continued on about the greatness of America and the Democratic Party.

By the end of the luncheon, my father was slurring his words and embracing everyone. Sammy Davis, Jr., who was an amateur photographer, aimed his camera at my father and snapped his picture. My father embraced him, too. I wished I could snap my own picture of the two of them—a man with an eye patch taking a photo of a man with an eye patch.

I helped my father to his car and rode home with him and my mother. After staggering into the apartment, he fell down in the hallway outside the living room and started shouting at my mother: She was ruining his life; she never wanted to go out; she was always sick and unhappy. My mother retreated to another room. Though I knew they didn't get along, I had never seen him yell at her like this. Trying to quiet him by saying how well he'd spoken at the luncheon, I managed to drag him to bed. Soon he fell into a deep sleep. I unlaced his shoes and slipped them off.

"He doesn't mean it," said my mother as I was leaving. "He had too much to drink. I'll fix him something good to eat when he gets up."

After the election, my father and mother were invited to the White House numerous times, something my mother liked to boast about. She was usually able to summon up the energy to attend. My father developed a special closeness with Humphrey, and did all he could to help get him elected president in 1968. He was greatly disappointed at Humphrey's defeat.

My mother kept a photo album of the 1964 luncheon and of their subsequent visits to the White House. Years later, after Ellen and I were divorced, I noticed that in one photo from the luncheon her face had been scissored out. My mother's memory was selective.

***

At camp I played the lover in a production of The King and I. *Henrietta Markowitz was Tuptin, the girl I loved. Henrietta had studied singing. Her voice was so full and overpowering that when we sang our duets, "We Kiss in the Shadows" and "I Have Dreamed," she drowned me out. I didn't really mind. My role models were athletes; I wanted to look like Joe DiMaggio, not an actor. Vinnie, the director, was dark-haired, theatrical and somewhat effeminate. I knew instinctively that he was homosexual, but it was not something I could have put into words then. At the time, his theatrical flourishes simply fit with being involved in the arts, as opposed to being masculine and a good athlete.*

At fifteen I was still good at sports but had become chubby. I had peaked as a softball pitcher at about eleven and then stopped growing. Being the lover in The King and I was not as good as being a star pitcher, but it was the best I could do at the time. Anyway, Henrietta was not my type. She had curly, light brown hair and an affected, cultivated English manner. Besides, I was going out with Melissa Cohen, a cute blonde who was restricted to the chorus numbers because she was tone deaf. We danced close together at Saturday night socials and sometimes snuck out to the woods together with other couples after bed check.

I didn't have a bad voice and wanted to do well. During rehearsals Vinnie urged me to sing louder and to kiss Henrietta more passionately. I was embarrassed but, with Vinnie spurring me on, I tried. I remembered having been impressed and moved as a younger camper by performances of the older boys in Oklahoma and Carousel and I wondered if I would affect any of the younger kids the same way.

The night of the show, Nancy, the counselor who made me up with rouge on my cheeks and a little lipstick, said that with my bright coloring I would have made a beautiful girl. I wasn't sure whether or not to take that as a compliment.

Backstage before the performance I held hands with Melissa and told her I needed to get in the mood for my part and led her to a deserted spot behind the curtains, where I kissed her and pressed her close. Just then Vinnie rushed past. He stopped and winked at us.

"So you do know how to kiss. Let's see some of that on stage," he said.

The king was acted by Arthur Fagan. He was fat and forceful, so his own personality fit the part of an imperious ruler. Later he went to Harvard College and Harvard Law School. During the performance on Saturday night the white powder in his hair filled the air whenever he shook his head, getting a laugh from the audience.

The show was a big hit and the cast took many bows at the end. I didn't stand out, but I hadn't been laughed at, either, so it was all fine with me. I just wanted to look cool. Afterwards, Melissa and I met in the woods. I smoothed the blanket on the ground, turned off my flashlight, pulled her down, and made out more seriously than I ever had before. I was sorry Vinnie couldn't see me.

***

Ellen and I attended several New York meetings being held in preparation for "Freedom Summer," in 1964. SNCC and CORE would be sending thousands of volunteers to Mississippi to get involved in establishing community centers, teaching, organizing, and encouraging voter registration. I had the summer off from my junior high school job, and several of our friends were planning to volunteer, so it seemed like a good thing to do.

We had an apartment on West 87th Street. Ellen was working occasionally as a freelance copy editor but the rest of the time she floated through her days without getting much accomplished. She slept late, talked to friends on the phone, drank coffee, smoked cigarettes, and read until two or three in the morning. She rarely cleaned the house or shopped or cooked dinner. In the morning when I rushed off to teach in the Bronx, she'd be sleeping. I wanted to shake her awake and tell her to get moving, but I knew that if I did we would just end up spending several days not talking to each other. I hoped going to Mississippi would give us some common ground and help us to get along better.

I wanted to volunteer for voter registration, which I imagined would mean riding around on dirt roads and listening to old bluesmen play in juke joints. But then the teachers' union offered to sponsor me by providing a monthly stipend and a rented car, so I ended up going as a teacher, even though I'd had a difficult first year in my own classroom.

At the end of June Ellen and I drove to Memphis for the orientation sessions, which were at the Lorraine Motel where, four years later, Martin Luther King would be assassinated. I was twenty-eight, older than most of the other volunteers—college students full of enthusiasm, ready to chant and demonstrate at the slightest opportunity. At the orientation we practiced passive resistance, acting out mock dramas in which fellow participants yelled at you while you refrained from yelling back or getting angry or even having eye contact with them. I followed instructions, somehow confident I would escape danger. It was the same way I had gotten through basic training, never believing I'd have to experience actual combat.

I felt like this despite the fact that three other volunteers, James Chaney, Andrew Goodman, and Michael Schwerner, had disappeared the week before we got to Memphis. Everyone talked about them nervously. When two lanky young men in Stetsons appeared one day at a workshop, they were rumored to be Southern infiltrators. It turned out that one of them was Harold Ickes, Jr., the son of Franklin Roosevelt's Secretary of the Interior. Subsequently that summer Ickes was beaten so badly by a gang of whites that he had to have his spleen removed.

Ellen and I were assigned to Meridian, where Chaney, Goodman, and Schwerner had worked before their disappearance. I was to teach a high school-level English class to black students at the Freedom School we had set up; I struggled to put together a curriculum based on ideas about racism, starting with Orwell's *Animal Farm* as an example of how one group could gain control over another. The kids were good students, the kind who liked school to begin with and were hungry to learn, but I was not a gifted teacher. It was hard for me to get ideas across and keep things lively in class.

During the first week a few Jewish volunteers tried to go to Friday night services at the temple in Meridian but were asked to leave. The local Jews were afraid of what would happen at the end of the summer once the outsiders had left. Many of the young volunteers didn't understand the complexities of racism in the South. They would stage spontaneous demonstrations in downtown Meridian. The newspapers referred to us as communist agitators. All it took to anger the locals was for a white and a black to walk together on the street. Once I was standing at an intersection with Ellen and one of my students when a car veered toward us. We jumped back onto the sidewalk. I don't think the driver was seriously trying to hit us, but he was letting us know how he felt.

The well-entrenched system then in place gave white Southerners a power over the blacks that they didn't want to lose: They were angry at the outsiders who were threatening the system and their power. And in fairness, many of the volunteers, myself included, suffered from self-righteousness and hypocrisy. True, we in the North didn't have separate black and white drinking fountains or bathrooms, so our segregation wasn't as evident, but we lived separately in our own cities and our schools were separated according to color and class. In many cases the whites and blacks in Meridian saw one another every day and knew one another better than we did in New York, even though the racism of the South was more open.

But more to the point, and something I could barely admit to myself, let alone anyone else, was that the deep, irrational anger I felt toward Ellen was similar to what Southern whites felt toward civil rights workers and blacks who didn't know their place. I wanted to intimidate and dominate her the way my father had dominated my mother, the way whites had ruled blacks for centuries. At times I almost felt sympathetic toward their position of wanting to control blacks.

I wanted a traditional wife, which Ellen was never going to be. When I first met her she had her own tiny studio apartment in the East Village, working when she needed to. After we got married and moved to the Upper West Side, things didn't change. Sometimes she talked of writing a mystery novel, or of studying psychology so she could become an analyst, but she got only as far as reading Freud and Jung. Ellen was quite intelligent and, I was certain, capable of doing anything she wanted to. The problem was that she didn't really want to do anything. She embraced the counterculture that we read about in *Rolling Stone,* loved the Grateful Dead and talked of living on a commune.

But once we reached Meridian Ellen began to thrive. Most of the volunteers liked to hang out at the center and drink coffee till all hours. This suited Ellen, who was a night person. She got right to work using her skills as an editor on the center's weekly newsletter. Often she worked very late co-editing the paper with Peter, a Princeton student. He was too sweet and innocent for me to be jealous, but I resented Ellen's late hours. In Mississippi she became alive and active, but not in the ways I wanted. Free of the routines and restrictions of our married life, she would stay up late with her new friends, talking about the problems of the world and how to solve them. One day when I was at a loss for what to do in class she came and spoke about how in the South the agrarian way of life had been used to create social and economic inequalities. I was proud of her—she was much more interesting and effective as a teacher than I could be—but I was also irritated and jealous.

When we returned to New York at the end of August I put Mississippi out of my mind and went back to teaching junior high school. Ellen resumed her unhappy, depressed existence. The next year we had a son, but she found the demands of motherhood difficult. Frequently when I got home in the late afternoon I would have to go out again to buy milk or bring pizza back for dinner. She sank deeper into depression, and the more depressed she became, the angrier I grew. Going to a psychotherapist didn't help her. Looking back I can see now that she was close to a nervous breakdown, but I viewed her depression as if it were aimed at me.

Meanwhile the South underwent some changes for the better: Many of the outward manifestations of racism disappeared. Freedom Summer had been a success. But our marriage drifted along until it ended seven years later, both of us still stuck right where we'd been in 1964.

***

The first time I actually had sex was after the "King and I" summer at camp. A few of us were walking along Amsterdam Avenue one night. Richie Lavigne, who had recently been expelled from military school, kept shouting, "Eat me, I'm a whoopie pie." In my innocence I pictured him as a sort of giant Yankee Doodle waiting to be consumed. Soon Richie was approached by a Puerto Rican prostitute. After he negotiated a price for the five of us, we all went back to her room in a nearby tenement. Each of us entered separately, while the other four waited in the hallway and peeked through the transom.

When it was my turn I walked into the room, past a pot of beans on top of the stove and over to her bed. She had a tired face and red lips, and she was lying on her back wearing just a brassiere. I was with her so briefly it seemed over before it had begun, and she called for the next boy to come in. So this was sex, I thought. After everything I'd read in books, I was a little disappointed.

***

In January 1965 Ellen and I, driving downtown, stopped for a red light at Fifty-Third Street and Seventh Avenue. Three black men were standing at the corner trying to hail a cab. One of them was Malcolm X. We had both just read his autobiography and had become admirers. "My God, look, it's Malcolm X," I said. I wanted to tell her to roll down the window and offer him a ride, but I was too intimidated by his fierce reputation to say anything.

Malcolm noticed us looking at him. Raising his hand, he smiled and waved, the way a young child does, with tiny motions of his fingers. I couldn't tell if he was being friendly or making fun of us for staring so openly. Then the light changed and—too flustered even to smile back—I drove off. I'm sure he would have refused to ride with us for security reasons, but I've always been sorry I missed the opportunity to say something to him. A month later he was gunned down in Harlem.

***

In January 1952, five of us seniors, honoring a hallowed Hudson School tradition, got an advance look at the geometry finals by bribing Tyrone, the janitor. Geometry was taught by Doc Stevens, a caustic and serious teacher whose standards were higher than most of the other instructors. He didn't put up with misbehavior in class. When we joked around, he'd silence us by saying things like, "The loud laugh betrays the vacant mind." Everyone knew that he kept in his desk a bluebook containing the final exam questions.

Tyrone was a tall, wiry, light-skinned black man who made periodic visits to the basement during the day to check the furnace and sneak sips of whiskey. He wore gray-striped, denim coveralls and a white T-shirt, a forerunner of how civil rights workers looked a decade later. Tyrone was no civil rights worker, though. He was simply bored with his work and so had started stealing exams for my brother's class four years earlier.

For a small core group at Hudson —to which I belonged— cheating was a way of life. Instead of studying for exams, we prepared intricate and tiny crib sheets, which took just as much effort, except that we felt studying was for saps. Once, on a school-wide intelligence test, I copied answers on the mathematics part from Julius Spellman, the class genius. I wasn't good in math and had no desire to be. But because we were seated alphabetically, Spellman was next to me, and it seemed wasteful to pass up the opportunity to profit from this circumstance. I received the second highest score in class and afterwards was often told that I was an underachiever.

We also misbehaved outside of school, walking up Broadway, shoulders hunched, looking for girls; hanging out on weekday afternoons at the 85th Street bowling alley and betting on games. On weekends we crashed parties and tried to disrupt them.

We made fun of other kids for studying and, when we tired of that, we teased each other. Our parents showed little interest in us. Nowadays our families would be considered dysfunctional. At the time they seemed normal.

Mr. Berenberg and Mr. Hall, the co-headmasters, were elderly men whose careers as educators had peaked years before. Now they weren't able to compete with modern, progressive private schools like Horace Mann and Dalton. Only a few serious students like Spellman wanted to study Latin and Greek with Mr. Berenberg, or 17th and 18th century English literature with Mr. Hall. The rest of us preferred to clown around or daydream in class. Once, looking out the window at the brownstone across the street, I noticed a young man in an undershirt sitting at a desk, reading a book and taking notes. He appeared to be in his mid-twenties, with dark hair and muscular arms. I imagined that he was studying to be a doctor or lawyer; I envied his seriousness and focus. After that I watched him frequently and wondered if he was aware of us.

One cold evening in late January the five of us met Tyrone at the entrance to the school, handed him five dollars apiece and, guided by the beam of his flashlight, followed him up the stairs to Doc Stevens' classroom. Tyrone shook a large ring of keys, moving quickly and drunkenly as he searched for the right one. He opened the top drawer of Doc's desk and pulled out the bluebook. Taking a few sips from Tyrone's bottle of whiskey, we copied the questions quickly, ran down the stairs, shook hands with Tyrone, and went to my house, which was the closest.

Once we began reading the questions we realized that we wouldn't be able to solve the problems by ourselves. We decided to call Spellman and offer him the exam for free in return for supplying the answers. He came right over and breezed through the questions. I think he agreed to help so that we would treat him as a friend instead of making fun of him as we usually did. And indeed we played up to him now and cheered him along. "Way to go, Julie baby," we said. "What a brain." We slapped him on the back and told him he was a genius. I copied down the answers, but didn't have the foresight to ask him for logical places to make mistakes so I could avoid suspicion by keeping my grade down.

We took the test the next day. Everything seemed to go smoothly, but the morning after, in the middle of our first class, the five of us were called in separately to see the headmasters. Two of my friends had already confessed, Mr. Berenberg told me when I walked in. A neighbor across the street had noticed a flashing light the night we were there, and phoned the school the next day to inform them of a possible robbery. As soon as Mr. Berenberg and Mr. Hall heard about our perfect scores on the geometry exam, they instinctively understood what had happened. I wondered if the call had come from the young man across the street.

I confessed immediately, but left Spellman's name out. Somehow none of us mentioned him; later he was admitted to Yale, a great achievement for Hudson.

My friends and I were suspended for a week before retaking the exam. Not surprisingly, I had trouble with it, but managed to sneak *enough looks at my neighbor's booklet to get a passing grade. Although I think Doc Stevens saw me, he just shook his head. By then the school had had enough of me and wanted me out by whatever means it took.*

Tyrone had to repay the money but wasn't fired. For the next few months the five of us stayed out of trouble and we were all admitted to college. Before graduation we met Tyrone in the basement to celebrate and presented him with a pint of whiskey.

At NYU I continued to cheat. Near the end of my first semester the English professor allowed us to write an original short story in place of our weekly theme. I lifted one from the Horace Mann high school literary magazine, for which I received a B-plus.

It was in my junior year course with Baudin, Jr. that I began writing my own stories. His praise of my writing made me realize, for the first time in my life, that cheating wasn't nearly as satisfying as doing the work myself. But in the last semester of my senior year, in order to graduate, I had to take a basic science course. I wasn't interested and didn't study. During the final exam I copied a few answers from the student next to me, the way I had in geometry.

Seven years later when I was teaching in the Bronx and taking City College courses to get a license, a professor during one exam walked out of the room for a few minutes. Most of the students (themselves teachers, of course) opened their textbooks to search for answers. My book was on the floor but I decided to let it stay there.

***

In 1969 I quit my job and enrolled in the MFA writing program at Columbia, hoping to continue the outpouring of writing that had been coming out of me in the early morning before driving to the Bronx to teach. But after a few weeks I realized that I wasn't going to be able to write at home. Every time I sat down at the desk in the dining room Ellen (hardly an enthusiastic housekeeper) began vacuuming. We weren't getting along; spending more time together didn't help. My plan was to write for three hours a day before afternoon classes, starting at nine after I'd taken my son to kindergarten at P.S. 84, a few blocks away, between Columbus Avenue and Central Park West. The neighborhood, in the midst of a large urban renewal project, was filled with deserted tenements. The new buildings were supposed to have special units for the local residents, who were being displaced, though eventually very few of them were able to remain.

But I wasn't thinking about the low-income residents being squeezed out of the neighborhood. I was just worried about a place to write in, and ended up renting a room on the tenth floor of a residential hotel owned by a Japanese company. A tall, narrow building on Riverside Drive and 80th Street, it was filled with Japanese students and young professionals.

My room was tiny, with just a single bed and a desk and a wooden chair. But it had a view of the Hudson, and the flow of the cars on the West Side Highway sounded like the ocean. I'd look out the window and, soothed by the traffic sounds, I'd forget everything and start writing, mostly stories about seductive, slender Japanese women. I became so excited that I had to urinate often. My room had a door that led to a small bathroom shared with another tenant. The man in the other room also seemed to pee a lot so I had to listen constantly. Every time he flushed the toilet and slammed the door to his room I'd rush in to pee, afraid he'd come back and lock me out. Some days it seemed we were having a contest over who could pee more often. Once as I walked to the elevator I saw him entering his room. Thin and nondescript, he was wearing thick glasses and carrying a notebook.

Every morning when I arrived at the room and sat down at the desk I felt a sense of happiness and excitement. I liked looking out at the Hudson—I would close my eyes for a moment and pretend that the traffic noise from the highway really was the sound of waves breaking onto a beach. I felt as if I was becoming a writer. One night at dinner I was telling an old friend of mine, a lawyer, about how productive I had become. The next day he called to ask if Dave, a colleague of his, could share the room with me. Dave had a writing project and wanted to use the room in the late afternoon. Though I wasn't comfortable about having someone else in my private space, splitting the cost of the rent seemed irresistible, so I agreed.

A few weeks later the manager stopped me at the front desk. In broken English, and with the air of a man betrayed, he told me that I'd have to leave. "Your friend bring girls," he said. "Not that kind of place."

"But he told me he was writing," I said.

"No more room," he said. He held out his hand for the key.

Dave had been bringing girlfriends there, making me look like a procurer. Embarrassed by the thought of it, I handed over the key. With no place to go, I began spending time at Columbia in the study halls and at Butler Library. Soon I was writing stories about full-breasted Barnard girls. But sometimes, sitting in a crowded study hall, I'd think of the room on Riverside Drive with its view of the Hudson and the soft sounds of the highway and the flushing of the toilet. I'd wish that I could be back there, waiting for my neighbor to slam the bathroom door.

***

I entered NYU at sixteen, which was too young, especially for me, since I was naïve and forgetful to begin with. I would write down the room number where a final exam was scheduled, but always on some scrap of paper that I invariably lost; then I'd have to track down another student to find out where to go to take the test. I lived at home—everybody at NYU lived at home then—which, I'm sure, reinforced my immaturity. My mother expected me to join her every night for dinner. She believed that otherwise, eating the unclean food in restaurants, I'd be poisoned.

Unlike City College, which required applicants to take what were called New York State Regents Exams, NYU was considered a sort of second-rate college at the time, where almost everyone could be admitted. But of course that made it actually an interesting place, with evening undergraduate courses for older students who worked: My classmates included Korean War veterans and people like Mrs. Shine, a forty-year-old mother of two, who sat next to me in Freshman English. I'd never even heard of Freud until we discussed a selection in our freshman literature anthology, but Mrs. Shine had read all of his books.

Often I wandered around the Village by myself. In the evening people in apartments left their lights on and their shades open, which made it possible to peek at the high ceilings, antique furniture, and crammed bookshelves. I dreamed of getting to know someone who lived in the neighborhood. I browsed frequently in the 8th Street Bookstore, while cool-looking customers stood around conversing as if they were at a party. The clerks looked like writers and spent a lot of time making private jokes. I felt like the ultimate outsider, but I went there often enough to become familiar with the names of poets like Allen Ginsberg and Ted Joans, whose small press books were on display.

One day I bought a couple of paperbacks about existentialism, which I was studying in a philosophy course at NYU taught by William Barrett, an editor at the Partisan Review. He seemed very hip in those days—he told the class that he'd named his son "Bird" for Charlie Parker or maybe it was "Satchmo" for Louis Armstrong. Later, during Nixon's presidency, he became a neo-conservative. One of the books I bought that day was Nietzsche's Beyond Good and Evil. Another was an anthology called Existentialism, edited by Walter Kauffman, a well-known Princeton philosophy professor. Both books were published by Anchor, which was started by Jason Epstein, at the time considered the young genius of publishing. Twenty years later when we were introduced at a party, he looked around for someone more important to talk to. But at the time I bought his books I knew nothing about him or, for that matter, existentialism, except that it was all the rage and that it was a way for me to become cultured and thus escape my family's bourgeois background. At home, hoping to improve my mind, I would close the door to my room and listen to Beethoven string quartets and field recordings of blues singers.

I left the 8th Street Bookstore with my bag of books about existentialism and walked back for my next class to the Main Building, which faced Washington Square Park. I had to use the bathroom and before closing the door to the stall I left my new books outside on the windowsill. I felt I ought to be able to trust anyone who came in not to take them. After all, they were about existentialism, and anyone who took books of such a nature would be doomed to feel guilty for the rest of his life.

I heard the door to the men's room open, a urinal flush, and the door swing open again. When I came out the books were gone. I was shocked. How could someone stoop so low, I thought. But there was nothing I could do, except curse myself for my simple-minded innocence. I found it hard to concentrate during the class. When it was over I rushed back to the 8th Street Bookstore to buy new copies of the books that had been stolen. Anchor books were around ninety-five cents at the time and I knew I could ask my mother for extra money if my allowance ran out before the end of the week. I was relieved that the young woman at the cash register didn't seem to notice that I had bought the same books less than two hours before.

In the end I never read any of them or, for that matter, really got to understand existentialism, except that it had something to do with taking responsibility for one's actions. I didn't have the kind of mind to grasp abstract philosophical thoughts. Every time I started reading Beyond Good and Evil *I fell* asleep. But I still liked to look at it on my desk.

***

After a few months at Columbia I started writing exclusively at Lewisohn Hall, where I could look out on a small rectangle of grass and trees. I'd bring a notebook and a book to read for inspiration. Previously I had needed privacy, but now I was able to get a surprising amount of writing done with other people around. I was ten to twelve years older than the undergraduates in the University's General Studies division, at least the ones who frequented Lewisohn during the daytime. It was exciting for me to sit there and look around at all those young people fidgeting and studying with such energy and intensity. My five years of teaching—for which I hadn't been suited in the first place—

had left me exhausted. Having the freedom to read and write in Lewisohn was particularly exhilarating. And I enjoyed sneaking looks at the young women around me. Sometimes they even inspired my writing.

One day I was reading *Tropic of Cancer* while admiring a young woman with long dark hair who was chewing gum and reading a philosophy text, *Ethics and Morals*. After a while she stood up, slipped on brown-tinted sunglasses and began putting her belongings into her backpack. She was wearing a black sweater and had full breasts. Our eyes met; she smiled. As I watched her walk toward the front steps I imagined writing a story about her, in which I followed her out and introduced myself. Her name in the story was Madeline. When we reached Broadway she invited me to her apartment at 111th Street near Riverside Drive. Her roommate was home and Madeline made tea for the three of us. I sat in an armchair in the living room. Madeline and her roommate took their shoes off and sprawled on the sofa. Exams were starting soon, Madeline told me, and laughed. "They make me horny," she said. Her roommate laughed in agreement. "I know what you mean," I said, sipping my tea. "All that nervous energy. You feel you've got to do something with it." Soon, like characters in a Henry Miller novel, the three of us were in bed together.

I wrote the story quickly in my notebook and walked home, feeling guilty. I picked up my son and kissed him.

The next day I typed it up and showed it to Mike Shaughnessy, a classmate in the writing program. Mike wrote novels and erotic poetry. He had just published a few poems in *Screw* magazine. He read my story over beers in the Gold Rail, a bar at 111th Street and Broadway that is now a Chinese restaurant, where Mike drank every afternoon. He was from Patchogue, Long Island, but the more beer he had the more Irish he sounded. He was always short of cash and I often bought him drinks. I didn't realize at the time that he was an alcoholic. "They'll love this at *Screw*," he said. He gave me the name of his editor and I sent it off that afternoon. A few days later I received a letter accepting the story, along with a forty-dollar check from *Screw's* publisher, Wet Dream Press. It was the first time I'd ever been paid for a piece of my writing. The following week my story was printed in a section of the magazine called "My Scene," under the title, *Boning Up for the Finals.*

A year later, during divorce proceedings, my wife's lawyer brought a copy of *Screw* to court to show the judge "what kind of husband" I'd been. The judge dismissed the claim, saying that since I was a writer, this piece of fiction was not relevant to the case. I felt elation. The judge had called me a writer. For the rest of the day I paid scant attention to what was happening in the courtroom.

***

During Christmas break of my sophomore year at NYU, I accompanied my mother to a hotel in Hollywood Beach, Florida. We went at the urging of my father, who, I think, wanted some relief from my mother's constant depression and from my own critical attitude toward capitalism in general and him in particular.

Our first night in Florida when my mother went to bed soon after dinner, as she always did, I snuck down to the lobby, where I met some people my age and stayed out until dawn drinking with them. At the time I was leading a solitary, lonely life in New York, mostly reading at home and going by myself to movies and concerts. I felt envious of friends who attended out of town colleges. In the lobby that first night I became friendly with Alan Berkowitz, a cheerful, muscular Dartmouth student. We hung out together for the rest of the vacation, drinking late every night, much to my mother's dismay, but there was nothing she could do to make me stop.

In February I visited Alan at Dartmouth for Winter Carnival and got my first taste of out of town college life. Alan belonged to Alpha Delta, which was known as the animal fraternity house on the campus, and his fraternity brothers did their best to live up to their reputation. Alan was the token Jew in a group that seemed to come mostly from the far West.

One of Alan's fraternity brothers was a gymnast who liked to hang from window ledges for minutes at a time, scream out curse words and sing bawdy songs. Another fraternity member walked around during a party in just a raincoat and shoes. Every once in a while he'd flash open his coat and take a bottle of beer from an inside pocket. By the end of the second night I was ready to come home.

That summer my parents rented a house in Atlantic Beach, not far from where Alan lived in Far Rockaway. Most nights we hung out at Lou's, a bar near the ocean. It was always filled with college kids in short-sleeved shirts and loafers, drinking Sea Breezes and Orange Blossoms. When the bar closed at three we all drove home.

One night, after I'd had a couple of drinks, I went outside to urinate because there was a long line at the men's room. I stumbled over to some scraggly bushes behind the building and relieved myself. When I got back Alan pointed to my feet and started laughing. I was wearing only one shoe. I shook my head and walked outside again, searching through the sand and the bushes, but couldn't find my other shoe. Finally, I drove home without it.

The next morning when I told my father, he burst out laughing and called a couple of friends to tell how his son had come home missing a shoe. For years after, whenever we had a few drinks together, he would repeat the story. I felt it was the first time he approved of something I had done.

***

In the middle 1970's Richard Elman, my old writing teacher at Columbia, wrote an article in *New York Magazine* about spending a week in the mental ward of Bellevue Hospital. He said they gave you pajama bottoms with no tie, so you had to walk around holding your pants up, which took away your dignity.

He always had to tell people he was not the critic Richard Ellman with two "l's", who had written the definitive biography of James Joyce, but Richard Elman with one "l," the novelist and author of non-fiction books. In his twenties he had been the program director of WBAI, where he produced radio documentaries, which, he said, taught him how to write novels. Richard was six feet four and, in a disheveled way, dashing and handsome. He liked to start conversations with women in the street. Once, standing next to him in an elevator, I watched him touch the arm of a young woman in a leopard skin coat. I was wondering if that was your real skin, he told her. She smiled back. But he had trouble with women who reminded him of his mother. There was an older female student in the course one semester: Whenever she spoke Richard was rude to her.

But when he was on, he was an inspiring teacher. After you left class you wanted to rush home and write. Individual conferences were stimulating and funny. In class he told stories and jokes and talked about books he had read. He had once tried being a standup comedian (though, as he told us, he had "bombed"). Often he gave us strips of paper with prophetic quotes from famous writers. While I was at Columbia, several of my best stories were inspired by things Richard said.

At the time he was getting divorced from his wife, Emily, a painter, with whom he had a young daughter. Two years later when I was going through my own divorce, he told me he'd fix me up with some Barnard co-eds, which somehow never happened, but the offer cheered me up momentarily.

For a few years after that, Richard lived with several roommates in an apartment connected to a psychoanalytic group known as the Sullivanians. They were a sort of cult that followed the teachings of one psychoanalyst and his staff of advisors. Many members of the group were in training to be Sullivanian therapists; they lived together in communal apartments on the upper West Side. Followers were encouraged to sever ties with their families. They were constantly making appointments to meet one another for half an hour at a local bar, where they talked about things like the weather and then moved on to the next appointment. They threw large parties at which people kept arriving like salmon swimming upstream until there was no more room for anyone. Sex between patients and therapists was permissible.

Some of Richard's roommates were also divorced, with children who would visit them at the apartment. After my divorce he invited me to join him there if someone moved out, a frequent occurrence. "It's a good place to work things out," he told me. "We have weekly meetings to discuss things, like sharing food in the refrigerator. You can stay here a year or two until you reach another level and then move on."

"But I've got a seven-year old son," I told him. "I don't want to move on. I want a permanent place for him to visit."

Over the years Richard's books sold less and less until finally his publisher, Scribner's, dropped him. The Sullivanian advisors held a meeting with him and ordered him to stop writing and publishing for five years. Richard immediately left the group and moved to a small studio on 76th Street between Broadway and West End Avenue. By then I was directing the Writers-in-Life program, sending writers to work with public school students. I hired Richard to do some workshops.

One afternoon when he had invited me over for tea, he got into bed and asked me to join him. He said he was lonely and wanted to cuddle with someone. I told him that the idea made me feel uncomfortable. After talking awkwardly for a while we shook hands and I left.

Over the next few years I occasionally ran into Richard in the street. He had remarried, as I had, and was teaching at the State University at Stony Brook. Looking older and tired, he complained on one of these occasions that the college wouldn't let him reduce his teaching load to part time so that he could start collecting Social Security at an earlier age.

 Some years after that I went to a theater on the Upper West Side to hear a reading of short stories in a series called Selected Shorts. One of Richard's was on the program, which I was enjoying, but I was irritated that my view was being blocked by a very large man seated directly in front of me. At intermission, looking for Richard, I finally spotted him with his wife. He had gotten heavier and seemed prematurely aged. It was sad to remember first meeting him thirty years before when he was so youthful and vibrant. I introduced him to my wife Alice. "Richard's a wonderful teacher," I told her. "He tried his best with me, but he couldn't do miracles." "No, no, you did all right, you were pretty good," he said as we walked together back to our seats. It wasn't till he sat down right in front of me that I realized it was Richard who had been blocking my view. That was the last time I saw him.

A few summers later in Vermont I was shocked to come across his obituary in the Times. He had died of lung cancer at sixty-three. A new book was scheduled for the following spring. When it was published I went to a memorial for him at Barnes and Noble. His daughter, now in her mid-thirties, thin and beautiful, was sitting near me. People came over to reminisce about Richard and she seemed pleased to hear all the sweet things they were saying about him.

***

Because I was so young when I started college I felt I had all the time in the world. After classes I hung out at the cafeteria drinking coffee and then went home to eat dinner with my mother. Many well known writers were appearing in the university's lecture series, but I rarely bothered to go. In my freshman year I missed hearing Dylan Thomas, who died the following fall. In four years I managed to go to only two lectures.

The first writer I heard was W.H. Auden, who gave a long, boring talk about writing lyrics for an opera. The second was Norman Mailer, who at the time had just helped to found The Village Voice. *He was a lot more stimulating than Auden. Instead of reading from a prepared text he responded to questions from the audience. At one point he explained that he had modeled the structure of* The Naked and the Dead—*in which alternating chapters were from the viewpoint of different characters—on* Anna Karenina. *I was startled to discover that writers actually had to learn their craft, and could be influenced by others. I wanted to ask him how he had started writing, but I was too reticent to raise my hand.*

Years later almost at midnight in a paperback bookstore on the Upper West Side, I found myself standing next to Mailer. We were the only two customers. He stared at me with what I thought was hostility. This was right before he stabbed his wife Adele. He seemed like a different man than I remembered from NYU.

***

Whenever Bernard Malamud came to New York, a friend of mine and her husband would arrange a poker game for him. My friend was one of his former students. When she invited me over to play one evening I was delighted. I admired Malamud's first book, *The Assistant*, for its warmth and its simple, Yiddish-sounding rhythms. As it turned out, Malamud looked and talked as if he could have been one of my relatives—He came on like a self-assured, somewhat cynical businessman, with a balding head and a thin mustache. For the first few hours, while his luck was bad, he said little and kept folding early. He refused to chip in for pizza since he wasn't going to eat any. Finally, when his cards improved, so did his spirits. By midnight he had drawn a little ahead. "It's time to turn in," he said with a laugh. "I've got to get up early tomorrow and write great literature." And then this man, the man who had written *The Assistant*, was gone. Where, I wondered, had he left all his warmth and humanity?

***

By the time I was nineteen I wanted desperately to learn to drive, but driving seemed an adult activity, like getting married, something I had doubts I'd ever be able to pull off. I craved a driver's license as much as anything I had ever wanted, except perhaps to sleep with a woman I loved, which also felt unattainable. My girlfriend had broken up with me the year before and I still thought about her.

This was the summer between my junior and senior years. I also wanted to get out of New York and see the rest of the country. I applied to the New York State Employment Agency to follow the harvest as a farm worker, something Mr. O'Rourke, my history teacher years before at Hudson, had told me about. *After one look at my camel's hair coat and white bucks, the interviewer at the employment agency advised me that this wasn't a job for me, that none of the farm workers could even speak English. I left disappointed. I had already imagined working my way cross-country, getting up as the sun rose every morning to pick vegetables and running into my ex-girlfriend in Texas, where she just happened to be driving by with her mother on a hot summer's day. When she saw how strong and sunburned I'd become, she would fall in love with me again.*

Now I dreamed of driving cross-country, but there was no one at home to help me learn. A few years before, my father had gotten a license at the age of forty-seven, after failing the driving test several times. On the third or fourth time, on the advice of his driving school instructor, my father placed an envelope containing a twenty-dollar bill on the passenger seat. At the end of the test the envelope was gone and my father passed. But his driving skills proved so limited that he soon hired a chauffeur. My brother, who was an excellent driver and would have helped me learn, was in the army in Oklahoma.

When I heard about a forty-lesson AAA driving course, I immediately applied. Bill, the instructor, was in his mid-thirties. He was one of those well-spoken and charming people who made you wonder why he wasn't working at something more ambitious.

I was in search of a father figure to guide me and responded well to anyone who filled this role. The year before, while I had been developing an interest in classical music, I was befriended by a young man named Cliff, who worked at Herman's, a record store on West 48th Street. Cliff guided me each week up the ladder from Tchaikovsky symphonies to Mozart and Beethoven string quartets. After I'd known him for about a year he went on vacation to Europe. When I went to see him soon after he was expected back, Herman, the owner, a voluble and outgoing man, brought me to his tiny office in the back and told me that Cliff had caught a virus on his trip and died in a hospital in Ireland. This was the first death of an adult whom I knew well.

So when I met Bill I particularly appreciated his friendliness and encouragement. Each one-hour lesson was usually shared with another student. Bill often praised me. "Look at how smoothly he's doing it," he'd say to the other student as I maneuvered into the correct lane before making a turn. I drove cautiously, for which Bill especially praised me. "Examiners give young people a hard time," he said. "They're looking to fail them the first few times to make them drive safer."

My father was skeptical about my passing the exam. He offered to give me an envelope with money in it to place on the passenger seat, but I refused.

Bill came with me on the day of the test, waving encouragement as I turned on the ignition. The examiner, a dour, middle-aged man, barked out his orders: Turn left at the corner, make a right, back up to the lamppost, park in the middle of the block in that space on the left. I followed his commands slowly and precisely. To park, I inched into the spot, carefully turning the wheel back and forth (this was before power steering) until I stopped equidistant between two cars, having made a perfect landing a few inches from the curb.

A week later I received my license in the mail. My father couldn't believe I had passed on the first try. He seemed disappointed that I hadn't needed his help.

When I called Bill, he congratulated me. "I'm not surprised. You're a good driver. And you're a smart young man. You should be able to do anything you set your mind to."

Bill was right about driving. I've always felt in control when I'm behind the wheel. A number of times I've avoided accidents by anticipating someone else's dangerous maneuver. I wish I could say the same thing about the rest of my life.

***

I once had my fifteen minutes of fame—six or seven minutes actually—when I appeared on the *Good Morning America* show to talk about Writers-in-Life. This was in 1975 or '76. I wish I had asked for a tape at the time, just as proof that it really happened.

I got on network TV by default. At the time Mitch Greenberg, a young, unknown writer was heading a Writers-in-Life project that taught fourth and fifth graders to write and produce their own comic books. I admired his drive and imagination, but not his outsize ego. He seemed sometimes appreciative of the financial and administrative support we provided him, but with Mitch there was never enough. To give him his due, though, the project was a great success. Dozens of students created comics several times a week. It took discipline and hard work and concentration, yet many kids begged to continue during their lunch hour or after school. The director of the foundation funding Writers-in-Life was so pleased at what she saw when she visited that she asked us to come up with another, similar project that they could support the following year.

Often I felt more like a business manager than the director of an educational group. Walking around during the day or traveling to work in the subway, I found I was surprisingly adept at working out budgets in my head. When we sat around writing the original comic book proposal, I'd mainly been interested in how many days each artist would teach and what the printing costs would be. When educational values were discussed—things like focus, concentration, better attendance and behavior, teamwork, writing and art skills, critical thinking—I tuned out. My long-term goal was to raise enough money to enable a group of writers to make a living wage, and thus create a community of writers/educators. Sometimes I had the feeling that I was back in the dress business, working for my father and brother, showing them how skillful I could be in practical matters, except that I could only allow myself to compete for money when I was doing it for a "good cause."

Mitch knew how to push for publicity. He helped get several articles about the project published in local papers. In addition, the mother of one of the boys in the class was a writer for *Good Morning America*. She managed to schedule an appearance on the program for Mitch and her son.

One winter morning at seven I turned on my TV and waited two hours to see them. But they never made it on. The featured guest that morning was Golda Meir, then the Prime Minister of Israel, and she was so mesmerizing that David Hartman, the host, interviewed her way beyond the allotted time.

Mitch sulked in the studio, then refused the director's invitation to return the next day. In the afternoon Josh's mother called and begged me to come on instead. "But I'm not a teacher," I told her.

"You're the director," she said. "That's even better."

I hesitated. I wanted to be on national television, even if I didn't feel I deserved it, but I was afraid of making a fool of myself. Finally, I couldn't resist; I told her I'd do it.

My apartment was just a few blocks away from Josh and his mother. She arranged for us to drive down together to the ABC Studio at Amsterdam and 67th. Before sunrise the next morning I got into the ABC limo and headed downtown to pick them up. She thanked me repeatedly for agreeing to come. Too nervous to talk, I just kept nodding.

At the studio we sat in armchairs in the lounge and drank coffee. Doris Kearns Goodwin, whose book about Lyndon Johnson had just come out, was sitting nearby. She was accompanied by her husband Richard Goodwin, who had been one of President Kennedy's bright young men in the early '60s. Dark-haired and slightly sinister looking, he whispered in her ear in a Svengali sort of way.

After a while an assistant led me to the makeup room, where I sat in a barber's chair while a man in a white apron looked me over. I was dressed in an open shirt and a sport jacket. My hair was long and messy. "Not much we can do with him," the makeup man told an assistant as he brushed powder on my face. I went back to the lounge and, with Josh and his mother, watched the show on a big screen. Finally, at around a quarter to nine, after Kearns Goodwin and someone else had been on, Josh and I were ushered onto the set. David Hartman smiled in a friendly way as he sat down opposite us. He was tall and oozed confidence and warmth.

"We'll be on shortly," he said. "I'll just ask you both a couple of questions. It'll be a snap. You've got a great story to tell."

Then the lights got brighter and the cameras zoomed in on us.

I felt like I was about to be executed.

"Some wonderful work is being done in a New York City public school," Hartman began and asked me to describe Writers-in-Life.

I rattled off a couple of sentences about the organization, something I did all the time when I visited foundations and corporations. Then I named all the writers involved in the project—Hartman rolled his eyes slightly at that, but I could feel my voice become stronger as I spoke.

Hartman asked me about the violence he'd seen in some of the comics the kids had produced. Weren't we just encouraging delinquent behavior?

I explained how much discipline and focus it took for kids to create their comic books, how they cooperated with one another as they worked and how many of them stayed during lunch hour to write and draw. Wasn't this the opposite of delinquency? I asked.

Hartman seemed pleased with my answer. He held up Josh's comic book and asked him to describe making it. I glanced around at the cameras. Suddenly I loved the lights shining in my eyes and the thought of several million people watching me. I felt as intensely alive as I'd ever been. Later Hartman asked me a few other questions, which I answered easily and smoothly. Then the interview was over and he thanked us, and both Josh and I walked off the set. Josh's mother hugged him and then kissed me on the cheek. "You were both great," she said.

I rushed downtown to the Writers-in-Life office in the Village, where the phone was soon constantly ringing. Mitch's call was first. "You weren't bad," he said, and then started complaining about Golda Meir again. My brother phoned to tell me he had watched the last couple of minutes after a friend had called to tell him I was on. "You looked great," he said. A little later the secretary from the company across the hall came in to let me know she'd seen me. I felt famous.

At eleven that morning I had an appointment in midtown with the corporate contribution officer at the International Paper

71

Company. I bounced into her office and started talking. "Did you see me on *Good Morning America* this morning?" I asked and described how much fun it had been and how proud I was of what Writers-in-Life did. I had never before been so full of confidence and energy talking to a potential funder. The program officer was a pleasant young woman who seemed to enjoy listening to me. A month later she sent Writers-in-Life a check for five thousand dollars.

By then I'd come down from my euphoria. For a couple of weeks I waited for someone to call inviting me to be on another show. Now that I knew I could handle those bright lights, I felt ready for them. It's been more than thirty years and I'm still waiting.

***

My father and his internist, Victor Scharfman, were close friends. They both had difficult, impossible wives; my father slept with models and buyers, while Dr. Scharfman had a longtime affair with his nurse, Miss Johnson. Dr. Scharfman was genuinely fond of Miss Johnson, a situation that never occurred in the case of my father, who sometimes became infatuated with his girlfriends, but only for short periods of time.

Dr. Scharfman, from a poor Russian Jewish background, had gone to Cornell as an undergraduate, then served in World War II. Soon after his discharge he opened a practice with another doctor on 76th Street and Fifth Avenue. Rents were still modest. Many of his partner's patients were Orthodox Jews who sometimes filled the waiting room until it felt like a synagogue. Dr. Scharfman wore blue button-down shirts and bright solid-color ties. He had a thick black mustache that made him look like a socialist, which he had been in the thirties, though he'd never joined the Communist Party. Such a move would have cost him his seniority at Beth Israel Hospital, which is what had happened there in the '50s to Dr. Edward Barsky, who refused to reveal the names of contributors to a fund that had sent Lincoln Brigade volunteers to fight in the Spanish Civil War.

When I was a teenager, Dr. Scharfman was the first liberal, sophisticated person I ever spent time with. He would talk to me for a long time when I went for a checkup, telling me Yiddish jokes and making references to writers and plays and politics. I think he sympathized with my artistic leanings and knew that my father wouldn't understand them. His own daughter was painter; one of her large still life canvases hung behind his desk. Later she became an art critic and wrote for the Partisan Review.

During my visits Dr. Scharfman would talk to me as if he had all the time in the world. He was the first person to inform me that Hemingway was an alcoholic, something my NYU professors hadn't mentioned in my American literature courses. At the time I was eighteen and when I described some of my hypochondriacal fears about dying he recommended that I go to a psychiatrist. Until then, embarrassed that I might be thought of as crazy, I had never revealed my problems to anyone. Though the psychotherapist proved to be unhelpful, I appreciated Dr. Scharfman's acceptance and sympathy.

In the early '60s Dr. Scharfman moved to a large apartment on Central Park West, with the assistance of a loan from my father, which was probably never meant to be paid back. Now that they lived near each other Dr. Scharfman came frequently on house calls; on occasion he would sleep over when my father felt seriously ill. As a cardiologist Dr. Scharfman was particularly devoted and attentive after my father suffered several heart attacks in his seventies, from which he eventually recovered. At 82, Dr. Scharfman had his own heart attack. After he returned to his office I asked him—I was still one of his patients—if he had thought about retiring, but he said there was no reason to. He liked his work. And he still looked good in his blue shirt and bright solid-colored tie. His mustache was now white, but he remained trim and sturdy. A few years later on his way to a conference at Beth Israel he had a fatal heart attack in the subway. I felt sad that his last moments were spent among strangers, but he died on his way to work, which was, I imagined, the way he wanted to go.

My father turned down the chance to say something at Dr. Scharfman's memorial service. Public speaking was sometimes stressful for him, though he enjoyed the attention, but this service was to be held in a small auditorium at the hospital and I think my father felt it wasn't worth the effort. Dr. Scharfman's wife and daughter asked me to speak in his place. They invited me over to the apartment on Central Park West and showed me letters patients had written to him over the years, which they thought I could use in describing him. Mother and daughter seemed to have a difficult relationship and while I was there Leila criticized her mother frequently. It was obvious that she had favored her father, for which I couldn't blame her. Mrs. Scharfman, a nervous, suspicious person, reminded me in many ways of my own mother.

When I spoke at the service, I strung passages together from the patients' letters, which offered a clear, consistent, sympathetic portrait of Dr. Scharfman. He had been a serious gardener: Several patients thanked him for the cuttings he'd given them of plants from his country house. Many of the letters referred to his good spirits, his sense of humor, his interest in them— the same qualities I had sensed in him. Someone told me afterwards that among the tributes that day, my speech had offered the best portrait of Dr. Scharfman. I felt pleased that I had repaid—in some small way at least—the gratitude I felt toward him.

I also wished I had been less restrained during those years when I'd seen him at his office. Dr. Scharfman knew about things that interested me, in a way that my father wasn't sophisticated or open enough to be curious about.

Though I had always, in my youth, been looking for sympathetic adults, I had missed, at least to some extent, the opportunity to learn from Dr. Scharfman, and to know him better. Perhaps it was because of his closeness to my father that I didn't reach out to him.

***

Anthony Bellone and I grew old together. When I was about 38 my previous shrink, whom I had been seeing for a year, suddenly decided to move to California. He wrote down the names of three psychotherapists to check out. I chose the first one on the list, Anthony, and then stayed with him on and off over the years from a combination of loyalty and lethargy. I wasn't sure if he was any good or not, but rather than try someone else I felt it was easier to keep seeing him, the same way I stayed with my Chinese laundry, even after they lost several shirts and the ones I got back often had wrinkled collars.

At the start of a session Anthony would sit back in his leather armchair, taking sips from an enormous mug of coffee, which he kept refilling. As the hour progressed, he'd become more animated. "You've got all that anger inside," he'd shout after I had related an experience where I felt mistreated. "You're afraid of letting it out."

In one way I agreed with him. I did have anger, particularly at my father, whose failure to understand me combined with his own success I found difficult to deal with. But I didn't feel at ease with the way Anthony kept pushing me to defend myself. Often I would leave a session angry with him only to come home and let it out by criticizing Alice. "What goes on there?" she would ask. "What does he say that makes you so angry?" I told her not to take it personally, that I was just working on my anger in general.

I wanted there to be some middle ground in my life, so I could stand up for myself when I felt it necessary, but in a reasonable, calm way, rather than building up to the kind of frenzy that characterized my sessions with Anthony. I tried to explain this to him, but he dismissed my words. "You're not facing up to it," he said impatiently. To help me understand what he meant, he told me about the time he had started to back into a parking spot; three young men pulled in from behind and blocked him, then dared him to do something about it. Anthony opened the trunk of his car, took out the tire iron and threatened them with it. They left in a hurry, he boasted.

"I wouldn't do that," I said. "I don't want to get killed over a parking spot."

"You're afraid to let your anger out!" he shouted.

The argument continued through the next session as we shouted back and forth. At one point he claimed that I had called him an ignorant Italian. (His mother came from Sicily and had worked as a seamstress.)

"What are you talking about?" I asked. "I never said anything about you being Italian. As far as I'm concerned everyone in New

York is Jewish."

"Alright, forget that," he said.

But as we continued to argue I wondered if, surrounded by patients and drowning in caffeine, he had lost his own sanity. At this point I had been seeing Anthony on and off for seventeen years, in which time he'd gained about thirty or forty pounds. Often while I waited in the small anteroom I would hear him shouting at someone, usually with increasing shrillness, as if he were trying to build each session to a kind of Greek tragedy climax. And lately during my sessions, he had started picking up the phone when it rang, rather than leaving it to the answering machine. "I'm expecting a call," he'd say as he shot up from his chair. Once, after saying hello, I could have sworn he was copying down a recipe for chicken cacciatore. Another time, when I tried to discuss the difficulty I was having with my writing, Anthony dismissed my complaints.

"You have to do research before you write," he said. "Your style is too obscure. It can't all come out of your head." I wondered how he could know this since he had never read anything of mine, claiming he was too busy. Finally, during the middle of one of our arguments, I told him I was quitting.

"You can't quit," he said. "You need me." He looked like he was about to cry. I felt bad for him, but I still insisted that I was going to leave.

"Come back one more time," he pleaded, which I agreed to do.

At our final session he told me again I was making a mistake; I didn't understand his methods. He even yelled at me a couple of times, but I sensed his heart wasn't in it. At the end of the session we shook hands. The next day I sent him a check.

***

One sunny, summer afternoon in Vermont I was sitting at the kitchen table, with a cup of tea, when I looked out the window and saw seven or eight cows near the plum tree. They looked big, almost like bulls, and were moving about uneasily. I hoped the farmer down the road would notice that some of his cows were missing. The low wire fence to his pasture had always looked flimsy to me, but the cows seemed like such gentle and contained creatures, as they ate grass and swatted flies with their tails, that I had never imagined them running away.

Petrie, the farmer, was drunk most of the time, or at least had a buzz on. Often I'd see him drive his tractor, with a wooden cart attached to it, to a field at the end of the road, where he kept bales of hay. He'd load some on and return to the farm, all the while sipping a can of beer. Relatives living in a rundown trailer next to his house helped him with his chores.

Sometimes Petrie's cousin, an older man, was the one who drove to the field for hay. He had long flowing white hair and sat perfectly straight, turning his head from side to side as he drove. If I was sitting on the deck he'd wave to me and I'd wave back, the way everyone does in Vermont.

The cows grazed near the plum tree for a minute or two before trotting leisurely around the house in single file. Then, still in a line, they moved to the dirt road and trotted back to the farm, stepping easily over the low wire fence and into their pasture. They looked like they had never left. I felt as if I had dreamed the whole thing up.

I walked out to the plum tree. Indentations from their hoofs were everywhere in the grass. These cows really had been there.

III

One Saturday morning I visited my father before he went to the racetrack, as he did on most weekends. *He asked how my writing was going, which surprised me, since he didn't usually show much interest.*

"I'm trying," I said. "I hope something comes, maybe a book eventually."

"Well, you're a smart fellow," he said. "You could write something as good as the crap that's in bookstores."

That was the closest thing to encouragement that he'd ever given me about my writing—I could write a book equal to all the trash that was being published. He meant it as a compliment.

At the time I was 40, divorced from Ellen and had just broken up with a girlfriend. My father opened a drawer in his bureau and took out a glossy picture of a woman in a low-cut dress, the kind of photo you'd see in a tabloid. "Would you like to go out with her tonight?" he asked. "You could come along with Sally and me to El Morocco." The woman in the picture was beautiful in a Hollywood way: lots of makeup, and shiny blonde hair that fell to her shoulders, not the kind of woman I usually dated or even thought about. I had a feeling we wouldn't have much to talk about, but since I wasn't doing anything that night I was tempted.

Then I thought of my mother in the kitchen preparing breakfast. How could I go out on a double date with my father and his mistress? Anyway, my clothing wouldn't be right. My best dress-up outfit for my job at Writers-in-Life was a sport jacket with a blue denim shirt and brightly colored tie. At El Morocco I'd look like a poor relation next to my father in his custom-made suit. I also knew I'd be nervous and tongue-tied.

"No, I can't make it tonight," I told him. "But thanks for asking."

From the kitchen my mother shouted that breakfast was nearly ready. We sat down in the dining room and the maid served us scrambled eggs.

A couple of years later I did publish a book, made up of autobiographical stories. In one I speculated on my mother and father's marriage, but didn't mention his girlfriends, or my mother's reclusiveness and her increasingly strange behavior.

I was still trying to come to grips with my feelings about my father. I loved him but I was also overwhelmed and somewhat afraid of him. Everything I did seemed dwarfed by his success and power. When I gave him a copy of my book he asked jokingly if Doubleday was the publisher. No, I told him, it was Release Press, a small independent literary publisher. He laughed at the name and the obscurity.

Still, I think he was a little intimidated. After all, he was in the book, and there were hints about the bullying side of his character and his need for power. On the other hand, I couldn't be sure he actually read it. Soon after I had given him the book, he met a friend of mine in the street and asked her if he was in it. "Well, yes, I think you are," she told him. Later she asked me how it was possible he didn't know. "You even use his name," she said.

As a young man my father had read Anna Karenina in Russian and then again in English when he came to America. In his early twenties he'd also read Dreiser's An American Tragedy, which he could still discuss in detail. Growing up in Europe he'd studied the Talmud and memorized considerable portions. He still loved to display his knowledge of it. He had a photographic memory, but once he started working in the dress business his reading stopped. As he grew older, friends sometimes gave him books as presents, often on philosophical and historical subjects, but he never got past a few pages before falling asleep. His reading days were over, except for the Times and the New York Post.

In his last years, though, he often introduced literature into our *conversations, perhaps trying to make me feel accomplished.* "Who are the important American writers?" he would ask. I'd mention Melville and Hawthorne and James and Twain.

"What about this century?" he'd ask, and I'd say Hemingway and Faulkner. He had once met Hemingway in a café in Cuba and he would describe how drunk Hemingway had been at eleven in the morning.

Then the next week he'd ask the same question and I'd repeat my answer, maybe adding a name or two. I enjoyed being the expert in these conversations since, when it came to the things he was good at, like business and money, I knew nothing.

In the late '80s, right after my mother died, I published another book, which described my parents in more detail. Fearful that my father would be offended, I didn't give him a copy. But a friend of his saw one in a bookstore and told him about it. "You didn't tell me you'd written another book," he said, and asked for a copy. After he read it he didn't comment directly, but advised me not to show it to my brother because one story contained a critical description of my brother's apartment.

By then my father was nearly ninety, but he still asked me questions about literature. And he often asked me to tell him again about George Orwell's essay "A Hanging," in which the condemned man jumps over a puddle on the way to be hanged in order not to wet his feet—Orwell's way of showing the cruelty and barbarity of executing a healthy human being.

And every week or so my father would call to ask me the name of the Norwegian author of the play about a town that tries to protect its image by concealing the fact that its water supply is poisoned. "Henrik Ibsen," I'd say, "An Enemy of the People." He had read it as a young man and the message had stuck with him. "Ah, yes," my father would say. "I always forget. I'll have to write it down." But the next week he'd call again and ask about it.

I didn't mind. I was happy to be of service to him. He was lonely, I think, and enjoyed talking to me. It had taken us a long time to reach that point.

***

My mother had been sleeping in my old bedroom since I left my family's apartment in the early '60s, because she had to get up frequently to go to the bathroom, which woke my father. Or so she said. By that time my father rarely spoke to her. My mother was still a beautiful woman, with smooth skin and delicate cheekbones. She was five feet three but over the years had become smaller and thinner. During the day she rested in bed, aided by a bottle of sleeping pills she kept nearby. The only person she talked to was her maid Mildred, a sedate churchgoing woman who wore a black wig. It was a great blow to her when Mildred, who was in her late seventies, the same age as my mother, retired to care for her invalid husband. Jackie, a young, sweet Haitian woman with lots of patience but little knowledge of English, replaced her. As time passed Jackie became depressed over the fate of her family and friends caught in Haiti's political turmoil, and she and my mother often sat at the kitchen table and spoke to each other of their woes, though they each understood little of what the other said.

Every few weeks I took my mother for a walk. She wore bright-colored shawls that she had crocheted and hats she shaped from silk fabrics. As she took my arm and walked unsteadily, she resembled a strange, rare bird that had wandered outside its natural habitat.

My brother seldom visited or called. He worked with my father and had no patience with my mother's physical complaints and her talk of dying, something she remained obsessed with over the last twenty years of her life. My father complained that she was interested only in eating and sleeping. He conceded that she had married him when he was poor and that she had been a loyal wife and had created a beautiful apartment for him. But what was the use of a nice home if he couldn't bring anyone there? The last time he had invited someone to dinner my mother spent a week supervising as Mildred shined the silver and polished the furniture.

Because my father and older brother were frequently out as I grew older, I had always been expected to eat dinner with my mother and keep her company. My father used to remark how much I loved her. I had mixed feelings. I knew how depressed she was, how confused and trapped she felt, and I sympathized—whatever struggle she and my father had waged at the beginning of their marriage, she had lost. But in my closeness to her, I felt like a loser too. After I became the director of Writers-in-Life, my father could never remember the name of the group or what we did. I made little money. Nothing I did impressed him. Next to him, with his hand-tailored suits and chauffeured car, I felt shabby.

So in 1982 when my mother called one night, as she often did when she was alone, I felt irritated. While she talked, I kept reading the magazine I was looking at. Why was it always me, I thought, and not my father or brother? They were too busy, of course, to play nursemaid. I grunted now and then as she spoke, to signal I was listening. But after a while I sensed a special urgency in her voice and put the magazine down. She kept repeating how much she loved me, that I was the only one who understood her and that I was too good for the world and should try to avoid being hurt by it. These were things she often said to me, but now she kept repeating them, her words coming slower and slower. And then her voice faded and stopped. "Mother," I shouted, but she didn't answer.

I took a cab to the apartment and found her sprawled on her bed with an empty bottle of sleeping pills near her head. My father arrived home from dinner soon after and we both rode in an ambulance to Beth Israel Hospital. Why would she do something like this, he kept asking. I wanted to tell him it was because of the way he had treated her, but I said nothing. The doctors pumped her stomach. She regained consciousness the next morning and recited a poem to me in Polish, translating line by line, about someone lying on the grass in the bright afternoon sun and watching the sky become dark and feeling the air become cold. Why, she asked, hadn't we let her die?

A week later she returned home. My father arranged for nursing care from early morning to midnight. I gave them my phone number. Two weeks later the morning nurse, arriving at

83

six, called to tell me she had just found my mother unconscious in her bedroom closet, with another bottle of sleeping pills at her feet. My father and I rode again in the ambulance to the hospital, where, once again, they pumped her stomach. This time when she awoke late in the afternoon she was quieter. "I guess I can't even kill myself," she said with resignation.

***

David Dubinsky, who later became the president of the International Ladies Garment Workers Union but at the time was a young organizer, helped my father get a union card as a cutter when he first arrived in New York in the 1920's. My father, who had been educated in yeshivas in Poland and Germany, wasn't happy as a factory worker. Within a few years he scraped up enough money to open his own dress contracting plant. He concentrated on the business end and left the production side to his forelady Helen, who for a time was also his mistress. During the Depression my father was behind on his rent, but at the beginning of World War II he made his arrangement with the head of the Woolen Bureau and procured his profitable contract to make WAC uniforms.

After the war he decided to become a manufacturer instead of just a contractor—He wanted to be the one designing dresses and selling them to the stores, rather than the one who had to knock at the manufacturer's back door begging for work. His first venture failed, but then in 1949 he succeeded, with an established manufacturer, Leonard Arkin and his son Andrew as partners. Arkin and Schrader did well, but Andrew, a few years out of Harvard and a champion bridge player, looked down at my father's European accent and asked him not to enter the showroom when important buyers were present.

Arkin and Schrader was located on the sixth floor of 530 Seventh Avenue, one of the premier buildings in the industry, and when my father finally had enough of Andrew's disdain, he took a small loft on the 15th floor and opened his own company. He had two minor partners, Marty Goldberg, a salesman with connections to the big department stores, and Izzy Silver, a patternmaker who knew how to grade sizes so that the dresses fit well. Marty was a formidable salesman and was able to place the company's dresses into the Fifth Avenue stores, but he had a weakness for women and ran up huge expenses. My father bought him out after the first year. By then he had eased himself into the showroom; he discovered that he could indeed talk to buyers and store presidents, take them to dinner and socialize with them. Originally he had tried to name the company A. Schrader, which he felt had an elegant sound, but a tire company in Brooklyn was already called that, so he settled for Abe Schrader, which in the long run proved a better name. "Abe" had an ethnic feel to it, implying a knowledge and skill at sewing and production, which turned out to be the strength of the company. The dresses were well made and fit comfortably. They were cut on the ample side so that heavier women felt good in smaller sizes than they could have fit into from other companies.

Izzy Silver oversaw production and, like my father, worked hard and enjoyed his financial success. At the age of fifty he learned to drive and bought a large Cadillac. But he was only five feet four and found it hard to see out the rearview mirror, even sitting on a cushion. He had to turn his head constantly to check on the traffic behind him, which resulted in several accidents. Years later Izzy retired to Florida and bought a Rolls Royce, which he rarely drove. It was kept wrapped in a plastic cover to protect it from dampness.

As his company grew, my father leased the entire 15th floor at 530 Seventh Avenue, but despite becoming a successful capitalist he retained his ties with the union. Frequently Dubinsky brought Democratic politicians to my father's showroom on their campaign visits to New York. When Lyndon Johnson and Hubert Humphrey became especially good friends of his, they both used him in speeches as an example of the American success story.

My father chaired dinners and fund raisers for Democratic candidates, like the one for Humphrey in 1964, and visited the White House frequently. According to him both Johnson and Humphrey and their cabinet, in fact almost all the politicians in Washington, liked to drink and have a good time. They also had extra-marital affairs.

Many of their wives and daughters and girlfriends came to my father's showroom to buy clothing wholesale. Even President Reagan's daughter Maureen bought dresses from him.

Bess Meyerson, the first Jewish Miss America, also frequented the showroom. She was known for reneging on her bills and was not allowed to leave with merchandise unless she paid cash up front.

In the televised 1984 vice-presidential debate, standing up against George Bush, Geraldine Ferraro wore an Abe Schrader beige tweed jacket with military braiding that gave her a strong, competent look. The next day the company switchboard was swamped with orders for it.

During his lifetime my father attended hundreds of garment industry dinners at the Plaza and Waldorf hotels, along with many weddings and bar mitzvahs. Women's Wear Daily quoted him frequently on industry issues and he served on the Board of the Fashion Institute of Technology. Mayor Lindsay appointed him co-chairman of the committee that changed the name of Seventh Avenue, between 34th Street and 42nd Street, to Fashion Avenue. He enjoyed meeting celebrities and people in power, and was never bashful about telling them of his accomplishments. He loved the attention.

***

Even after her second suicide attempt, my mother was unenthusiastic about seeing a psychiatrist. "Why should I pay someone just to listen to me talk? I'll listen to him and he can pay me."

My father felt the same way. He was critical when I arranged for a psychiatrist and then a social worker to visit her. They both made recommendations, in which neither my mother nor my father showed any interest. Part of their reluctance was a refusal to face up to their unhappy marriage, and part was their feeling that psychiatry was something frivolous compared to the necessities of life, like food and shelter. The social worker suggested sending my mother to an old age home, but my father wouldn't consider it. "She has a beautiful place to live in already," he said. "I would never send her away, no matter how crazy she is." He considered her suicide attempts some kind of momentary aberration.

My mother felt the nurses who attended her at home were an extravagance. "She does nothing," she said of one nurse who had been especially considerate and attentive to her, even buying her a tape of famous opera singers because my mother had told her of going to operas with her father when she was a young girl. "She's only doing this to get on my good side, to keep a soft job," my mother said.

Soon the nurses were gone and my mother was once more alone, except for Jackie, the Haitian maid. Jackie did her best with her limited English, but she remained depressed herself over the violence and poverty in her own country. My father took command again, resuming his distant and hostile relationship with my mother. He rarely spoke to her and could hardly bear to look at the wreck she'd become, as if her decline was her personal revenge against him.

Since my brother had long ago given up on her, I ended up being the only one who visited and talked to her. Yet I too felt an anger and impatience with my mother's refusal to acknowledge her unhappiness. "I've had a good life," she would insist when I visited. "Abe was a little tough sometimes but underneath it he was alright. He's given me everything I could ask for—a beautiful apartment, jewelry, fur coats. I've been to the White House and danced with President Johnson."

Mostly, she slept. She still took sleeping pills, the same ones she had used to try to kill herself with, but now Jackie kept the bottles hidden from her and doled the pills out and watched as she swallowed so my mother couldn't hide them.

"I couldn't even commit suicide," my mother told me. "I guess I'll just have to live to the end." She seemed resigned as she said this, a little smile on her face. "I'll have to wait until death comes and then I can rest forever."

I remembered how devastated I'd been after her first attempt. I'd cried in the hospital and then at home, thinking how sad her life had become, and I was angry with my father for his cruelty to her and his refusal to acknowledge her pain and depression. I tried to convince my mother that she had a lot to live for. She had two grandsons, and my wife Alice was pregnant. Maybe she'd have a granddaughter she could teach to crochet and knit and fashion the exquisite little dolls she had learned how to make from her father, who had manufactured braiding for uniforms for the Czar's army. But my mother said it was too late. She couldn't bend her thumb and her cataract operation had been unsuccessful, so she couldn't sew anymore.

I realized that nothing I could say would change her or give her relief. It had taken courage to swallow all those pills and perhaps it was unfortunate that she hadn't taken enough of them. Now she was imprisoned in a huge apartment for the rest of her life, without friends or love. Sometimes she forgot I was there and talked to herself about her childhood, remembering the rivalries with her two sisters. Her father had loved her more than them, she felt, and the two of them had gone to the opera together without her sisters. When I would arrive she'd raise her head from her pillow and tell me how happy she was to see me but soon she'd start talking about wanting to go to sleep forever. Her life was over, she couldn't even go shopping anymore. I'd tune out as she spoke and try to concentrate on something pleasant, mumbling a few words when there was a silence. Afterwards I'd take a long walk to clear my head.

***

Though he was always nervous about his accent, my father did love to give speeches in public. The occasions he spoke at were usually fundraisers for Jewish causes or garment industry dinners, and the audience was invariably friendly and appreciative. He had several stories and anecdotes that he frequently managed to weave into his talks. One went as follows: "Don't walk in front of me, I may not want to follow; don't walk behind me, I may not want to lead; but walk beside me and be my friend," which he attributed to Albert Camus, pronouncing Albert with a "t", and Camus with a long "a" and an "s." Another favorite of his was a story in which Nietzsche was arrested for something controversial he had written. He looks out his cell window, sees a bird, and says to a fellow prisoner, "I see an eagle. "But that's only a sparrow," the man says. "If I see an eagle," Nietzsche replies, "it's an eagle."

My father used this story to illustrate his belief in optimism, which he felt had been a key to his success in life. Neither writer had any connection to the words my father attributed to them, but in the 1950s he became enamored of the existentialism (or at least the idea of it) that had eluded me as an undergraduate; and he would throw around some names to make his own words sound more significant. He had a mistress named Rita who took philosophy courses at the New School and gave him books by Camus and Nietzsche, which he kept by his bed. Rita was an instructor at a Fred Astaire Dance Studio, where my father won several gold buckles in dance contests, with her as a partner. She was short and dark-haired, with bright red lips and a large bosom. After he'd been seeing her for a few years she became hooked on drugs and began calling him at home late at night, so he changed his number to an unlisted one, telling my mother that Rita was a disturbed woman whom he had turned down for a job. Then Rita appeared at his showroom one day, screaming to the receptionist that she wanted to see my father. He ushered her into his office and gave her money to get rid of her. That was the last he saw of her.

His next mistress Cindy was a young, blonde stewardess with a full, voluptuous figure. When my brother married a woman from Nice, my father took Cindy to France with him but made her wait in the hotel while he attended the wedding. The next day he and Cindy left on a trip around Europe, accompanied by a friend of his to act as his cover, just in case he met anyone he knew. This was at the time when my mother had grown too feeble and reclusive to leave the house; my father could use her illness as an excuse for his philandering. He liked to be seen in public with younger, attractive women and took them to expensive restaurants. Being with them affirmed his masculinity and youthfulness, the way that using Camus' and Nietzsche's words in his speeches validated his intellectual stature.

***

In the 1980s, first Dr. Scharfman, whom we'd known for fifty years, died, and then a niece of my father's, at fifty-eight. My mother shook her head. "How can I still be alive," she asked wonderingly. I continued to visit her every week and spoke often with her on the phone. One November afternoon six years after her second suicide attempt, she felt sharp pains in her chest. She told Jackie not to disturb my father at work, but when the pain increased Jackie called him. He and my brother rushed home from the office. By the time they went with her in the ambulance she had lost consciousness.

When I arrived home early that evening my daughter's babysitter told me excitedly that my mother had been rushed to the hospital. I was relieved that this time it was my father and brother who were with her and not me. I took my time getting ready—brushed my teeth and washed my face. I stuffed a paperback book in my pocket, took the subway downtown and walked east from Seventh Avenue and 18th Street to First Avenue, past a stretch of cast iron buildings that I liked. It was a route I had walked many times before when one or the other of my parents was hospitalized in Beth Israel. I got to the emergency room to find my father anxiously begging the doctors to use every effort to revive my mother. One of the doctors told my brother and me that she was clinically dead and that nothing would bring her back. But my father insisted they make an incision and massage her heart. After about ten minutes she was pronounced dead.

"I can't believe it," my father said as we drove uptown in his car to Riverside Chapel to arrange for her funeral. "Jackie should have called me right away. They could have saved her."

It was Thanksgiving Eve and the streets were jammed with spectators watching the floats being prepared for the parade. We had to get out of the car and walk the last few blocks to the funeral home. Afterwards we ate a late dinner at a luncheonette on Columbus Avenue. Then my brother went home. I walked back with my father and stayed with him that night to keep him company.

Before we went to bed he said, "I could have been nicer to her."

The funeral was two days later. A persistent rain fell and at the cemetery water ran down the hill, forming puddles near her grave. My brother and I helped my father keep his balance as he struggled down the incline. Many of our relatives were buried nearby, including my father's parents and my sister Estelle, who died at the age of seven the year before I was born. It was cold and raw and my father was shivering, though at the time I wondered if his discomfort came partly from the guilt he felt at the harsh way he had treated my mother. "I don't like the thought of being buried here," he said to me. "I can feel the dampness in my bones."

"I don't want to be morbid," I told him, "but when you get here you won't notice it."

***

My father loved action—usually revolving around money. At work he talked to his broker half a dozen times a day, interrupting a dress fitting or a meeting to find out how his stocks were doing. Once when I was around twelve, he came home on a Friday night just as my friends and I were in the middle of a poker game. The betting stakes were two and four pennies. My father sat down with us, joined the game, and bet the maximum on every hand. Within half an hour he had cleaned everyone out. He gave us back all the money and added an extra five dollars. Then, getting up, he said, "You still can't beat the old man," and went to bed.

When my father went to the racetrack he bet on long shots, often several in the same race. He'd sit at a table in the clubhouse having a sandwich and coffee with friends and getting tips from racing sheets and from acquaintances—someone who knew someone who knew someone who had heard from the vet which horses were healthy. At the last minute, right before the bell sounded, he'd place his bets, often adding an extra horse or two on a hunch. He got to know the ticket sellers and tipped them regularly, so he was able to arrange with some of them not to record his ticket number when he won big, thus avoiding some taxes.

He gave large amounts to charity because he understood what it was like to be poor, but also because he liked the attention and praise he drew. Often the honoree at dinners to aid causes for which he'd raised money, he was critical of other businessmen who didn't feel the obligation to give back.

In the '70s my father became known in the dress business as the Ultrasuede King. Ultrasuede was a synthetic fabric that looked like suede but could be cleaned in a washing machine. It was a time when air conditioning was starting to be used widely and women, particularly in the South, needed to cover their shoulders all year around. The company that made Ultrasuede rationed out a strict amount to its customers every month to keep the demand for it high. Everything my father produced in Ultrasuede flew out of the stores and it drove him crazy that he couldn't obtain more. Finally, he began buying the fabric from other manufacturers who weren't as successful with it as he was. He paid them a premium, of course, so they could make a profit, but that gave him enough to fill orders from stores like Neiman-Marcus, which kept begging for more of his Ultrasuede outfits. My father could never get enough Ultrasuede. It was like eating caviar, he said.

As he grew more successful, he started going to four-star restaurants like Le Cirque. When I ate with him there he insisted on betting each time on how many lumps of sugar were in the bowl on our table. He'd tell me to guess first and then he'd say a number. Invariably, he won. It took me a year or two before I realized that the headwaiter always whispered the amount to him beforehand. My father liked to bet on a sure thing.

Once, when he was in his early nineties, we drove up Eighth Avenue and passed the building on 38th Street where he'd been a dress contractor begging for work from manufacturers. "I wasted twenty years of my life there," he said, pointing to the building. He had waited a long time to reach the limelight and once he got there, he made sure to bask in it.

***

For a few weeks after my mother's death my father reminisced about her and seemed shaken. But then his spirits gradually lifted: he resumed going out every night with friends and enjoying himself as he always had. He led a vigorous life for almost thirteen more years, continuing to work every day and to go out to dinner with friends at night. Each year before Rosh Hashanah and Yom Kippur, according to Jewish tradition, my father, brother, and I visited my mother's grave in Queens. We'd stop at the main office, go to the men's room and then drive slowly along the cemetery road until we found the section where my mother was buried. My father would say a prayer and we'd put small stones on her tombstone. Then we'd walk around looking for other relatives.

The cemetery was old, filled with individuals who had originally reserved their spaces through burial societies, and the graves were squeezed together the way many of the dead had spent their lives. A majority of the gravesites weren't cared for; bushes and shrubs grew jungle-like between the monuments, often obscuring the engraved names. Estelle's tombstone was especially hard to find because it was short, carved like a tree cut down at the base to signify the briefness of her life. I liked discovering it each time and standing there for a couple of minutes. It was as if I was finally meeting up with Estelle and spending time with her, something I'd never had the chance to do in her life.

Though I wasn't religious, I looked forward to these visits. It was one of the few times my brother, my father and I spent time together without anyone else. We weren't much of a traditional family, didn't celebrate birthdays (except my father's) and didn't express feelings of love for one another. My father set the tone— He wasn't interested in the ordinary routines of family life, and family itself seemed to have little meaning for him, aside from his financial obligations. He was more focused on seeking approval and praise from rich and powerful people.

About five years later my brother and his wife bought burial plots in Sharon Gardens Cemetery in Westchester and my father agreed to be buried there also. My brother called to ask if I'd like to reserve space there too, but I told him I planned on being cremated. I resented my father's decision to abandon the cemetery in Queens where my mother was buried, but I didn't say anything.

My father gave his plot in Queens to his youngest sister Rae, who died two years later in 1998. She and my mother had never gotten along but now they would lie in the ground next to each other for eternity, while my father would rest in upscale Westchester.

***

When my father was fired at the age of eighty-eight by the large conglomerate that had bought his dress manufacturing company three years earlier, he began trading his stock portfolio full time. Now he talked to his broker dozens of times a day; the rest of the time he looked at the stock prices at the bottom of his television screen. Often during our conversations he'd hold up his hand to silence me while he checked the worth of a particular company and then placed a call to his broker to instruct him to buy or sell. The broker spent lots of time on the phone with my father but also made tens of thousands of dollars in commissions on his trades, while my father was satisfied because he felt in control of his own business affairs. Once he opened an account with the son of a friend of his at Sanford Bernstein, a prestigious and well-established firm, but then had to rely on monthly reports to find out how his investments were going. After six months he closed the account. "I can do better myself," he said.

When his broker retired in the early '90s, my father took over his desk and went down to Wall Street every day. He enjoyed the company of the other brokers and flirted with the secretaries. Each morning he stopped in the lobby to get a shoeshine from Tony, who called him by his first name; they traded stock tips. A few of the brokers were Orthodox Jews with whom my father liked discussing the Talmud. Once, after one of them had given him a tip that netted my father several hundred thousand dollars in profits, he showed his appreciation by making a large contribution to the yeshiva that the broker's son attended.

Everything went well until the late '90s when the market slumped and my father lost most of the profits he had made in the previous ten years. At the end of the day he'd call me to complain how much money he had lost. Once a week or so, he asked me to have dinner with him. My father's chauffeur would drive him over to my apartment around six. He would take me to an expensive restaurant and then drive me home. In the last years of his life we'd usually go to Elio's, an Italian place on the Upper East Side that he enjoyed. He ate early so that he could sit at one of the preferred tables in the front where regulars and celebrities ate in groups of three and four; after he left, the restaurant could still serve a couple of more groups at that table.

My father had a sensitive stomach and liked to eat simply. Each time he ordered he reminded the waiters that he didn't want his food cooked with oil or butter. "Now I know the chef is going to use oil," he'd say.

"No, no, Mr. Schrader," they'd answer. "We know, no oil or butter, and you want your noodles burnt." They seemed to enjoy his bantering, and they didn't mind the big tips he left. Giovanni, the maitre d', never refused the twenty my father slipped to him every night to insure that he got a table at the right location. The staff, like everyone else, was in awe of his vigor and clarity of mind and his zest for life, which was extraordinary for someone in his late nineties. As we ate our dinner, the surrounding tables would fill up with people he knew. He liked to table hop so he could chat with them. When he returned he'd tell me who they were and how much each one was worth. Many of my father's acquaintances were in real estate: Sometimes he would moan about all the opportunities to buy shares in office buildings that he had turned down. "I'm just a pisher from the schmatte business," he'd say, shaking his head. "I'm worth nothing compared to them."

"Well, at least you're sitting at a good table," I'd say, and he'd laugh. Because one of the owners of Elio's had literary connections, writers ate there sometimes. Once I saw Joan Didion and her husband John Gregory Dunne, and another time Arthur Schlesinger, Jr., who looked unapproachably stiff and self-important. One evening Lew Rudin from the famous real estate family and Burt Roberts, the Bronx District

Attorney who'd been the model for a main character in Bonfire of the Vanities, *came in with Sidney Poitier. My father got up to say hello and this time I followed him in order to meet Poitier, who was one of the handsomest and most charming men I had ever seen, equal to Cary Grant, who many years before I had glimpsed from a car window as he walked down a block in the East Fifties.*

Near the end of his life when my father lost some of his optimism he'd go on during our meal about the terrible state of the market and his investments. He told me he had lost somewhere between four and five million dollars. Half joking, I told him that meant my brother and I had each lost two and half million. I asked him why he didn't take his money out of the market and invest it in something safe and keep just a million or so to play around with. I didn't understand stocks very well, but I knew several wealthy people who kept most of their money in bonds. They looked at money the way I did, as something that gave them security and allowed them to do the things that they found important. But over the years my father had lost interest in everything that wasn't connected with actually making money. Even his involvement in politics, which he followed closely and was active in, was contingent on his being able to make big contributions and get invited to political events and meet senators and presidents. A million wouldn't be as much fun, he said. "Well, it's your money," I told him. And it was true, he had made it all himself, though I sometimes felt a little sad about that four or five million.

***

When Charlie Zimmerman died my father, who was ninety-one at the time, asked me to go with him to the funeral at Riverside Chapel. It was noon on a beautiful fall Sunday. We walked the few blocks from the apartment on Central Park West to the funeral home on Amsterdam Avenue. Charlie had been the vice president of the Ladies Garment Workers Union, and our neighbor years ago in Washington Heights. His son Paul was the same age as my brother and they had been good friends, though that was a long time ago. Charlie was a staunch union man who fought dress manufacturers like my father over workers' pay and benefits. My father respected Charlie but felt that his kind of philosophy would eventually drive everyone out of business. Once he sent Charlie four bottles of whiskey for Christmas; Charlie sent two back, with a note saying that two was his limit, a way of letting my father know that he couldn't be bought.

Riverside Chapel was crowded and my father made the rounds, greeting union members and friends from the garment industry. Then he led me to the back of the chapel and sat down on the aisle near an exit. "I'm going to slip out once the service starts," he told me. "A friend's picking me up to go to the track. It's a beautiful day. Charlie would have liked me to enjoy myself."

***

In 1987 I traveled with my father to Poland to visit Ostralecko, his hometown, which he hadn't seen in sixty-five years. None of the buildings he remembered were still standing, which depressed him, and we left early to spend a few days in Cannes, where he knew some people. Our first morning there he went to the lobby to change dollars into francs but decided not to, because the hotel's rates were high. "We'll do it in town," he said.

We took a taxi and rode for about ten minutes to a store that changed money. My father asked the driver to wait while he went in. Then we drove back to the hotel.

"How much did you save?" I asked.

"Thirty dollars."

"What did the cab cost?"

"Fifty dollars."

"So you lost money."

"It's not the money," he said. "It's the principle. You should never let anyone overcharge you."

***

Once or twice a month I used to visit my father before he went to the racetrack. I would sit with him while he ate breakfast and then dressed. One time he went to his closet, lifted out a wardrobe bag, unzipped it and took out a navy blue sport jacket. "How do you like it?" he asked. "It's made of vicuna wool. It cost fifteen hundred dollars. I've worn it maybe two or three times in ten years."

"Maybe it wasn't worth it, then," I said, with a touch of sarcasm.

"Well, I'm wearing it now," he replied, as he straightened the sleeve of the jacket over his cufflinks and admired himself in the mirror.

When he was ninety-seven he pledged five hundred thousand dollars over a four-year period to Beth Israel Hospital, which named its front entrance for him, with a plaque calling it the Abe Schrader Lobby. The fourth year was a terrible one in the market, and he could fulfill only part of the final payment. Jokingly, I warned him that the hospital could take down the plaque as easily as they had put it up. He just said they would have to wait; he'd pay it off the following year. But he died before that.

Diagnosed with cancer at the age of one hundred, he chose to have an exploratory operation rather than a colostomy. An operation, if successful, would have allowed him to keep working. The surgeon told me that older patients usually had the colostomy and afterwards stayed home and spent their remaining time with their families. But my father told him about the bad run in the market and said he needed a year or two to make back his money so he could take care of his boys, as he called my brother and me. "Mr. Schrader, you're one hundred years old," the surgeon told him. "Maybe your boys should take care of themselves by now."

It turned out that the cancer was untreatable. There were complications from the surgery, and he died a week later. He would have lived longer if he had left his illness untreated. But he was a gambler and preferred to take his chances.

My brother and I sent Beth Israel a check from the estate to honor his pledge, as we knew he would have wanted.

***

CODA

One of the last dinners my father attended was the one he gave himself at the Plaza Hotel for his hundredth birthday.

He asked me to write a speech for him. I had done this previously and felt I had a sense of his style. And I was happy to be helpful to him, since he was such a self-sufficient man. He seemed to have everything; even buying a birthday present was difficult.

The party was scheduled for a Sunday in mid-October, a day after his actual birthday. In July I went to Vermont and started making notes, so I could give him a draft when I got back in September. I wrote about how he forged his own papers and ran away from the Polish army when he was nineteen, ending up in Cuba, where he stayed for nine months and met some Jews who took a liking to him and got him Cuban papers under the name of Anthony Salgado, so that he could enter the United States. And I wrote how he had struggled as a dress contractor for twenty years, having to borrow money to pay rent on his business loft.

In the middle of July my father called. "How can you do this to me," he asked. "Leaving me without a speech for my party. Everybody will be there, millionaires, billionaires. I'll look like a dummy."

"Dad, it's only July. I'm working on it."

"Please, get it to me right away. I need it now."

A few days later I returned to New York, printed a draft in large type, and delivered it to him at home in the evening. He sat on his bed in his undershirt and shorts and read it immediately, correcting details as he read: He had come to America in 1921, for example, not 1922 as I had written.

When he finished he told me the speech wasn't bad, but that I should take out everything about Poland and Cuba and his early struggles in business. "No one wants to listen to that," he said. "They just want to hear about my success and how great America is."

I told him I didn't agree and that what he wanted to take out were exactly the things that made his life interesting. "But it's your speech," I said.

A few weeks before the party my father ate dinner at Elio's. Punch Sulzberger, the publisher of the *New York Times*, was at the next table. My father told him about the party and asked if Sulzberger could arrange for a write-up.

The next day a photographer and a writer came to my father's apartment and interviewed him. The day after he was the subject of "Public Lives," a column that at the time appeared daily in the *Times*. The first half of the article was about his life in Poland and then his journey to America via Cuba.

He called me that morning as soon as he saw the paper. "You've got to fix the speech," he said. "There's nothing in there about my coming from Poland."

"But you told me to take it out," I said.

"Well, put it back in. It's important. I need it."

He had invited two hundred and fifty people for the event, and he hired a party planner to advise him on all the details—the band, the floral display, the selection of speakers and, what proved most difficult of all, the seating plan. The ballroom was to be arranged in two parallel semi-circles of tables—but my father had to decide who should sit in the front rank. Most of the guests were rich and successful—in fact there was little room for relatives and old friends—and my father didn't want to insult anyone by putting him in the second rank, which he called "Siberia." Finally, with what seemed to me to be the wisdom of Solomon, he insisted on sitting in the back himself, thereby equalizing the ranks. After all, if the honoree sat in the second tier then it wouldn't be an insult to join him there.

About half a dozen people were asked to speak, including former mayor Koch. My brother and I also said something, mostly because the planner advised it. I felt nervous, as I always did, when I had to perform in front of my father and in this case compete with him—he took his public appearances seriously. My brother and I managed to get through our talks without mishap, but my father stole the show, partly through what he said and partly because he was unique, a one-hundred-year-old man with a clear memory of the times he had lived through.

He spoke for nearly twenty minutes, adding his own touches by quoting the Talmud from memory—in Hebrew—and throwing in quotations that he said were from Kierkegaard and Schopenhauer. The audience of several hundred listened closely to every word. Even the musicians in the orchestra seemed spellbound. Everyone listened intently as he reminisced about things like selling lemonade to the Russians in 1914 as they marched into his town. The Russian recruits didn't know their left from their right and wore a piece of straw on one shoulder so the commander could give instructions by saying, To the side with the straw, turn!

When my father finished he was showered with congratulations.

Well after midnight Alice and I rode home with him in his car and reviewed the evening. He kept asking me if he had spoken with an accent, something he was always concerned about. I told him, as I always did, that the accent had been part of his charm, but finally, to reassure him, I said it was so slight that you really couldn't hear it. Then he asked me for the tenth time if he really had been good.

I was hungry for some words of praise myself, particularly from him. "First tell me how I was," I said.

He shook his head dismissively. "You spoke too low. I couldn't hear a word you said. I was sitting in the back."

It was the story of my life, I thought. Then I told him once more how good he had been.

Soon after this party my father asked me what I would say at his funeral. At first I said I didn't want to think about it, that he would be around for a long time, but he kept insisting. Finally I told him I would say that he had come to America as a poor young man, with holes in his shoes.

"I never had holes in my shoes."

"All right, then, I'll say you started out as a cutter."

"Don't say I was a cutter. It's not a dignified profession."

"You know what," I said, "You give the speech."

When he died that summer, his grandchildren—my son and daughter, and my brother's son—spoke at his funeral. Neither my brother nor I felt up to it. My father was a hard act to follow.

#####